The Also Rans Series ①

RUN, JEREMIAH RUN!

D0168399

Mabel Elizabeth Singletary

MOODY PUBLISHERS
CHICAGO

All Scripture quotations are taken from the King James Version.

Editor: Tanya Harper
Cover Design: TS Design Studio
Interior Design: Ragont Design

Library of Congress Cataloging-in-Publication Data

Singletary, Mabel Elizabeth.
    Run, Jeremiah run / Mabel Elizabeth Singletary.
        p. cm. — (The Also Rans series book 1)
    Summary: Although he longs for a home and family, orphaned, nine-year-old Jeremiah finds it difficult to settle in the various foster homes in which he has been placed until, by default, he goes to stay with the family of his social worker.
    ISBN-13: 978-0-8024-2253-8
    ISBN-10: 0-8024-2253-5
    [1. Orphans—Fiction. 2. Foster home care—Fiction. 3. Interpersonal relations—Fiction. 4. Christian life—Fiction.] I. Title.

PZ7.S61767Ru 2008
[Fic]—dc22

                                                                                          2007050766

1 3 5 7 9 10 8 6 4 2

Printed in the United States of America

RUN, JEREMIAH RUN!

*This book is dedicated
to those who choose to live and run each day in faith.*

CONTENTS

Chapter 1

A BORN RUNNER

"HURRY! CATCH HIM! Don't let him get out of the area!" yelled Mr. Kelton, the school's principal, as he joined Mrs. Lane, the cafeteria lady, and Mr. Ray, the custodian, in an attempt to stop nine-year-old Jeremiah Jones from running through the lunchroom.

"I got him!" Mr. Ray called out as though he had scored the winning touchdown in the Super Bowl. Surprisingly, he had spoken too soon, because just as fast as he thought he'd grabbed him, Jeremiah's little honey brown hand slipped out of Mr. Ray's grip like butter.

"He's already in the hallway!" Mrs. Lane called out. "I can't believe this!"

And that was pretty much the way everyone at McArthur Elementary School felt when it came to Jeremiah. No one could recall ever meeting a child quite like him. When he moved, he ran. It was as if walking didn't exist.

From the moment he entered the building at the start of the day until it was time to board the bus for home, he ran.

He hadn't been a student at McArthur long, yet in less than two short months, everyone knew who he was. One reason for this was he could be heard coming long before you ever saw him. And when he ran, he didn't step softly. Each time his feet touched the floor, they sounded so loud it was surprising they didn't leave a permanent imprint. The rest of the students learned right away, if Jeremiah was in the hallway, the best thing they could do was to get out of his way.

Mr. Kelton entered the main office looking defeated and as though he had been caught in a whirlwind. His shirt was disheveled, and his necktie was draped behind his left shoulder. His face was red and perspiring, and in his rush past his secretary's desk, he slapped his hand loudly on its corner and shouted, "Get that child's parent on the phone!"

Mrs. Flint didn't waste a second in following his direction. Right away she looked up the number and contacted Jeremiah's foster mother, Mrs. Daniels, and proceeded to explain what had happened. "Yes, we need you come down to the school . . . no, we haven't been able to catch him yet. Yes, Mr. Kelton would like to speak to you. Hold on, please, while I connect you." She immediately pressed the button on her phone connecting Mrs. Daniels with the principal.

Just as Mrs. Flint hung up the phone, in walked the school nurse, Ms. Gregory, with Jeremiah in tow. She was steering him into the office and holding on to him tightly to make sure he didn't get away. She knew if she made the mistake of loosening her grip, he would soon be gone again. "Here's our little friend," she said, guiding him toward the secretary's desk. She wore a cool smile of content as though she had single-handedly solved a great mystery. She pointed to a chair placed against the wall and out of the way of office traffic. "Now, let's see if you can sit down. I'm sure your mother's probably on her way."

"So you caught our runner, I see," Mrs. Flint said with a sigh of relief. "I thought Mr. Kelton was going to come apart at the seams when the cafeteria called and said Jeremiah was on the run again."

Jeremiah sat in the chair he had been assigned, thinking it strange how people could so easily and comfortably talk about him as though he wasn't there. He gripped both hands tightly onto the arms of the chair and pressed his back against its soft cushion. As peculiar as it may have seemed, holding on the way he did helped him to stay put. He closed his eyes and concentrated hard in an effort to remind him to sit still.

Opening his eyes, he peered out the huge office windows in front of him and watched two robins swerve about through the air and smiled because he believed he knew how they felt. They were happy to be able to soar as they did without anyone's questioning whether their movements were right or wrong. To him, they were free, and nothing was better than the act of being free.

Maybe, he thought, *I'm supposed to run just like those birds are supposed to fly.* He couldn't understand why no one else could see and accept that. Silently he wished people didn't look at him as they did. He felt as if one day he'd landed in the middle of a place with a label stuck on his back that spelled out in bright red letters the word *"DIFFERENT."*

It wouldn't have been so bad if McArthur was the only

school that saw him this way, but the problem was more serious. Every school he'd been placed in since first grade pretty much saw him the same way. Now as a fourth grader, he was starting to wonder himself about why he couldn't just slow down and blend in with all the other kids. Why did this need to run seem to overtake him every day of his life?

While he sat, Mrs. Lane brought in the lunch he'd never gotten a chance to eat. He liked Mrs. Lane a lot. She was a rotund woman with a friendly smile. He thought it was funny the way she believed eating was a cure-all for just about everything. "Eat and you will feel better," she often said. And this time was no exception. "Here you are, Jeremiah," she said, handing him a small tray containing a peanut butter and jelly sandwich and a carton of milk. "Now you be careful not to make a mess and stay in that seat."

Jeremiah reached for the tray and placed it on his lap. He knew Mrs. Lane's words were not just those of gentle advice; they were also a warning.

"Oh, and I think this is yours too," she said, handing him a large notepad. It was thick with large sheets of paper and pictures drawn by Jeremiah. Almost all were pictures of superheroes. Some wore colorful capes that flew high above their heads, but all stood tall with tightly clenched fists and wore expressions that characterized their great power and authority. None of them wore masks like the ones he had seen in comic books. Jeremiah wanted the faces of the superheroes he drew to always be revealed. This way, there would be no need for any child to fear them, and the kindness in their eyes would be fully seen.

Trying to keep the tray on his lap, he smiled and held out his hand for the pad. "Thank you, Mrs. Lane." He placed the treasured pad behind his back, knowing it was secure. Balancing the tray on his lap, he quietly folded his hands, bowed his head, and silently said grace. "Amen," he said calmly. He could hear the voice of Grandma Joanie whispering in his ear. "Always give thanks, Jeremiah, for all that the Lord has provided."

All he had left of his grandma were her words. When he thought of her, good feelings flowed everywhere inside of him. When things happening around him seemed too difficult, he'd remember something she'd said. These were what he called *"strong words."* He called them that because, when they came to mind, he felt strong and believed he could make it no matter what the problem was. He missed his grandma but felt better when he thought of her in heaven. He pictured her looking down at him as a way of making sure everything was all right. He wondered if she missed him as much as he missed her. Nothing in his life had been the same since losing Grandma Joanie. Picking up half of his sandwich, he began to eat.

Mrs. Lane exchanged glances with the secretary, shook her head, and declared, "Guess he can't help it. Maybe he's just a born runner." As Mrs. Lane left the office, Mrs. Flint gave her a smile declaring that she understood.

Jeremiah had paid no attention to the conversation the ladies were having except for the comment about him being a born runner. *Maybe they did understand*, he thought. He looked out the window again hoping to see the robins, but they had flown away. He wondered where they would end up. He wished he too could take flight and land in a place where he could feel "normal." He knew that wasn't about to happen, so he dismissed the thought and instead focused his attention on a large spider scampering across the side of Mrs. Flint's desk.

Suddenly and without any warning, he leaped forward to swat at the uninvited creature. And when he did, his tray of food along with his carton of milk went flying into the air and noisily landed on the floor. Some of the milk even spilled onto some papers sitting on the corner of Mrs. Flint's desk. "Oh no!" she exclaimed. "What have you done now, Jeremiah? Just look at this mess!"

Jeremiah could feel everything inside of him coaxing and urging him to run, and run fast. He wanted to get as far away from where he stood as possible and as fast as his legs could carry him. He was already in trouble for the ruckus he'd caused earlier in the lunchroom. The absolute last thing he wanted to happen was for Mr. Kelton to come out of his office and see the latest mishap. Without hearing the order, he knew what was coming. He sat back down in the chair and bowed his head. "Sorry," he whispered.

To which Mrs. Flint gave no response. She had reached her limit for tolerating Jeremiah Jones for the day, even though according to the big clock on the wall, it was only five minutes to twelve o'clock. Instead, she got up from her desk, hurried over to the PA system, and grabbed the microphone. The announcement she made was heard over the entire school. "MR. RAY, YOU'RE NEEDED IN THE MAIN OFFICE. PLEASE COME QUICKLY!"

As she returned to her desk, she gave Jeremiah "the look." It was an expression he had seen so many times before in his young life. It was a look that clearly said, "Enough."

Almost immediately, the door to the main office was thrust

open and in walked Mr. Ray with a trash bag and a mop. Somehow he knew the announcement paging him had something to do with Jeremiah Jones. He also knew that if Jeremiah was involved, it meant there would be considerable cleaning up to do. "Gee, how did I know?" he said, picking up the food and placing it in the trash bag. "School ain't nothin' like it used to be. Back then kids were seen and not heard. If you gave 'em a direction, they followed it without question." Once he finished picking up the food, he mopped up the spilled milk.

Jeremiah wanted to help clean up the mess he'd made, but he knew not to move from his seat. He just couldn't chance making another mistake.

When he finished, Mr. Ray pointed at the floor. "There we are . . . looks good as new. Until the next time," he said chuckling and left.

At that very moment Jeremiah could see a black Ford sedan pulling up in the school driveway. He knew it was his foster mother, Mrs. Daniels. This would be her third visit in less than two weeks. To Jeremiah's surprise, when the car door opened, the situation suddenly got worse. Out stepped his foster father, Mr. Daniels, as well. Jeremiah knew that for both of them to come to his school, things really had to be serious. Not that he expected them to, but when Mr. and Mrs. Daniels entered the office, neither one of them was smiling. Still, the reality that confirmed he was in deep trouble didn't set in until they walked by and refused to look at him. There was something else he recognized, and it scared him. Mr. and Mrs. Daniels were wearing "the look," too. Once their meeting with Mr. Kelton was over, he was certain he would be on his way to another home once again.

Mr. and Mrs. Daniels walked toward the secretary's desk, and she wasted no time escorting them inside to speak with Mr. Kelton. Knocking on his door and then opening it she said, "Mr. Kelton, Mr. and Mrs. Daniels are here."

Jeremiah couldn't see Mr. Kelton but could hear his voice coming from behind the door and felt thankful that he sounded calmer than he had a short time ago. "Please have them come in," he requested. The door once again closed, and the meeting went on for close to an hour.

During that time, Jeremiah had taken out his drawing pad and sketched a bouquet of flowers for Mrs. Daniels. He planned to color them when he got home later that day. Her favorites were daisies, so he would use bright yellow to make them look like the ones she'd planted in the front yard. The drawing of the daisies would surely make her smile. And if she smiled, he knew everything would be better.

When the couple emerged from the principal's office, they looked solemn and worn. They each shook hands with Mr. Kelton and observed Jeremiah. In a weird kind of way, Jeremiah understood. He didn't blame anyone. He knew they had tried, and they had tried hard. The sadness in his eyes was clear, and no words were necessary. Mrs. Daniels took him by one hand, while Mr. Daniels took the other, and the three of them walked out of the office. Looking back, Jeremiah saw Mrs. Flint and Mr. Kelton standing by the window. They watched as the black Ford sedan pulled away from the curb. It was a scene all too familiar for young Jeremiah. As sure as he was of his ten fingers and ten toes, he was equally as certain he'd spent his last day at McArthur Elementary School.

GOING HOME

THE LONG RIDE was a quiet one. No one said a word. Jeremiah sat in the backseat of the Daniels' car with his face pressed hard against the window. He stared out at the changing scenery as they rode past unfamiliar houses, buildings, and a neighborhood park along the way. It didn't take long before he realized his prediction had been correct. The route they were taking wasn't the way to Mr. and Mrs. Daniels' home. He was pretty sure now that he was on his way back to Children's Services. Jeremiah wished he had the power to rewind everything that had happened since he came to live with Mr. and Mrs. Daniels, but was forced to accept that all the wishing in the world wasn't going to change the fact that he was losing yet another foster home.

Just for a moment, he allowed himself to go to a "safe place." He closed his eyes and tried to think of some of Grandma Joanie's *"strong words."* Jeremiah needed strength and picturing her words in his mind would give him that. He reached his right hand deep down into his pocket and closed his fingers tightly around a carefully folded piece of paper. Inside the paper were eight tiny mustard seeds that Grandma Joanie had given Jeremiah only days before she died. Listening in his heart and remembering her kind words was the one thing Jeremiah felt still connected the two of them.

Almost as if she was sitting beside him, he could hear her sweetly whispering, "If you have the faith of a mustard seed, God can move even the biggest mountains standing in your way." He never knew how she came to possess them, or even if they were real mustard seeds at all. However, there was no doubt they were of great value to her. And she believed in the truth she found in God's Word. So she often reminded Jeremiah that this was the source from which she found what he referred to as his grandma's *"strong words."*

To Jeremiah, the seeds were both a treasure that his grandmother had passed on to him and at the same time a reminder of what a powerful God could do if a person had faith. Closing his eyes and hoping for something to happen, Jeremiah repeated, "Faith . . . have faith . . . God can move even big mountains." When he opened his eyes, the houses, the buildings, and the road they traveled on were still unfamiliar to him. Nothing had changed. He was still riding in the backseat of Mr. and Mrs. Daniels' car headed for a place he didn't want to be, but he was powerless to do anything about it. Inside his pocket, he allowed his hand to release the paper that held the tiny seeds, let it descend to the bottom of his pocket, and accepted the likelihood that there would be no miracle for him today. Fitting himself snuggly in the corner of the backseat, he fell asleep.

It must have taken close to an hour to reach the red brick building bearing the name "Children's Services Office of Philadelphia." Jeremiah lifted his eyes acknowledging the fact that, even though a new sign had been placed on the front of the building, it was still the same place that in the past two years he'd been brought back to over and over again.

He could see Mrs. Kennedy, his social worker, standing out front waving to make sure they'd seen her. Mrs. Kennedy was very nice, and Jeremiah enjoyed being around her. She and her husband, Paul, had a son of their own named Paul Jr., who was about the same age as Jeremiah. They nicknamed him P.J. so that they would always know who she was referring to when they heard her call. Jeremiah had met him once when Mrs. Kennedy couldn't place him with a family right away and he stayed with them for the weekend. For two nights he slept in P.J.'s room and recalled how surprised and impressed he was when P.J. insisted that Jeremiah take the bed while he slept in a sleeping bag on the floor.

Mr. Kennedy was real nice, too. Jeremiah remembered how he played football with them on that chilly Saturday afternoon last fall. He thought of the fun he'd had that day and wished a time would come when he'd have a family of his very own, like the Kennedys. The reality though was that Jeremiah knew way down deep in his heart that he didn't just want to be part of a family like them; they *were* the family he wanted to be a part of.

As Mr. Daniels parked, Mrs. Kennedy stepped closer to the car. She bent down, peered into the backseat and waved hello to Jeremiah. He slowly and cautiously waved back and somehow managed to return a half smile. When he got out of the car, he threw both hands around her waist and hugged her tightly. It was as though he had been reunited with someone he loved and had greatly missed. He liked the way she smelled like fresh lilacs and wished he could hold on forever and never let go. He did everything he could to keep his tears from breaking through, but couldn't stop them. "It's all right, Jeremiah," she said. "It just wasn't the right fit. We'll keep trying."

Mr. Daniels took Jeremiah's suitcase out of the car's trunk. It was pretty easy to see by the shirtsleeve hanging out the side that the packing had been rushed. Everything that belonged to him was in that one suitcase, and he hated the sight of it. Seeing it reminded him that he didn't really belong anywhere or to anyone. He no longer had a place he could call home. But then again, he hadn't really had a real home since losing his grandmother a little over two years ago.

Mrs. Daniels reached out to give Jeremiah one last hug and returned to the car. She was crying and kept dabbing her eyes with a tissue. Likewise, Mr. Daniels did the same and hugged Jeremiah. "You'll be all right, Jeremiah . . . you'll be all right." Then he got back into the shiny black sedan, turned on the motor, and they drove out of Jeremiah's life forever.

Mrs. Kennedy took Jeremiah by one hand and pulled his suitcase with the other. "Wait 'til you see what I've got for you inside," she said sweetly. Jeremiah didn't hear her. Instead he watched the Daniels' car until it completely disappeared from his sight. "Oh, I get it, you're not interested," she said, trying to take his attention off of the departing vehicle.

"What?" he asked softly.

"I guess you didn't really like those chocolate chip cookies I made the last time you were here. I brought you some more, but if you don't want . . ."

Jeremiah remembered the warm scent of Mrs. Kennedy's freshly baked cookies and the way the smell so pleasantly filled his nostrils. So for a moment, he forgot about his situation and focused on the subject of cookies. "I want some!" Nothing came as close to the delicious taste of his grandma's secret cookie recipe except for the ones baked by Mrs. Kennedy. Next to Grandma Joanie's cookies, Mrs. Kennedy's were the best.

He looked up at Mrs. Kennedy and accepted that Mr. and Mrs. Daniels had become part of his past. Though he now wondered who next would become part of his future. For Jeremiah Jones the answer to that all-important question was waiting to be determined.

Mrs. Kennedy spent the rest of the afternoon making phone calls in a desperate attempt to find Jeremiah a place to stay. She knew what he liked and set before him a basket of colored pencils and drawing paper. He opened his pad to the page containing the bouquet of flowers he had drawn for Mrs. Daniels. Changing his original plan, he used various colors to complete his picture. He decided to give it to Mrs. Kennedy when he was done.

While he worked on his picture, he tried to ignore the difficult conversations bombarding Mrs. Kennedy over the phone. She wasn't having any success finding a solution to his problem. Before long it was five o'clock, and she knew there would be no placement made on this day.

Mrs. Kennedy made one last phone call. This one, though,

was very different from the others. She smiled and spoke softly to the person on the other end. When she ended her call with the words *"I love you,"* Jeremiah knew she was talking to Mr. Kennedy. "Okay, Jeremiah," she said rising from her seat. "Let's go! You're going to stay with the Kennedys for a little while. Is that okay?" Her words couldn't have made Jeremiah any happier. Even if it was only for a day or two, he knew it would be a fun one or two days and he looked forward to living them. Jumping up from his seat, he tore the finished page from his drawing pad. "It's for you!" he said, anxiously handing the bouquet picture to Mrs. Kennedy.

The time and care he had taken completing the picture was obvious. When Jeremiah drew, his hand was steady, and he gave all of his attention to his work. His pictures had to be "just right" before he'd offer them to anyone. She kindly accepted it and held the picture with both hands. She admired the drawing, and it made him feel good knowing she appreciated the gift he had created for her. "This is the most beautiful bouquet of flowers I've ever seen. And they look so real! Thank you, Jeremiah. And I just bet you're planning on become an artist someday. Am I right?"

Jeremiah shrugged his shoulders. He never thought that he could someday become a person who would draw pictures for a living. He loved drawing more than anything else in the world. There couldn't be any job better than that. Knowing that Mrs. Kennedy acknowledged his artistic talents made him feel important. Maybe he *would* become an artist someday, a great artist whose pictures would be displayed in museums all over the world. *Wouldn't that be wonderful?* Jeremiah thought.

Jeremiah handed the basket of crayons back to Mrs. Kennedy and attempted to help tidy up her office so they could leave. "Everything looks fine," Mrs. Kennedy said, giving her approval on the room's appearance. "I believe we can be on our way."

Jeremiah grabbed his art book, while Mrs. Kennedy once again pulled his suitcase by the handle. "I think I'll make something special for dinner tonight. Would you like that, Jeremiah?"

Jeremiah knew he'd like anything Mrs. Kennedy cooked, but he especially liked her pancakes. "Can we have pancakes with lots of butter?"

She looked at him kindly and attempted to get him to desire something more traditional for dinner. "I had planned to make them tomorrow morning for breakfast. There's nothing like hot fluffy pancakes early in the morning you know."

"I like them all the time," he responded.

"So does P.J. I guess it won't hurt to see what it's like to have pancakes for dinner."

"But if we pretend it's morning, they'll be just as good as when we have 'em for breakfast," Jeremiah offered.

Mrs. Kennedy paused to think about Jeremiah's suggestion. "I'm almost convinced, but I do have one condition."

"What's a condition?"

"I need you to do something for me."

"What do you want me to do?"

Mrs. Kennedy remembered how Jeremiah didn't like eating fruits or vegetables. She figured it would be easier if she tried to get him to eat some fruit first. "Will you eat the fruit I give you along with your pancakes?"

Jeremiah waited as though weighing the offer made to him.

"Deal?" Mrs. Kennedy asked.

"Will you make the pancakes real big?" he asked, forming a giant circle with his hands.

"Well, maybe not that big, but yes, I'll make them big," she said.

Without any reluctance, Jeremiah agreed. "It's a deal. I'll eat the fruit."

Mrs. Kennedy placed Jeremiah's suitcase in the trunk of her car and opened the rear door so he could sit in the back. "Mrs. Kennedy, are you sure it's okay for me to stay with you?"

"I'm sure, Jeremiah. And P.J. will be glad to share his room with you. He likes you, you know. And besides, I don't think you'll take up much space," she said, kidding.

Jeremiah felt at ease. "I won't," he told her. "I just need a little space, that's all."

She hadn't been driving for even ten minutes when she peeked into her rearview mirror and saw Jeremiah had fallen asleep. It had been another real long day in his young life, but for now he was sleeping peacefully. Mrs. Kennedy wondered if he was dreaming while he slept. And if so, what was this nine-year-old dreaming about? One time when she checked on him through her mirror, she thought she saw a smile of innocence spread across his face. She knew if he was dreaming, at least for those few short moments he was dreaming about something good.

They were almost there as she turned the corner and headed in the direction of her house. The Kennedys lived in a small well-kept bungalow type house with cream colored shutters framing each window. It was the last one at the end of a nicely manicured cul de sac. Jeremiah remembered the pretty flowers that adorned the front yard. They were bright, colorful, and welcoming. Pulling into the driveway, she silently prayed that Jeremiah would be able to be placed in a loving home real soon. He needed that, and more important, he deserved it. For now, she was glad that she and her husband and son could open their home for him to stay, even if only for a short time.

PLANTING

THE MOMENT Mrs. Kennedy pulled the car into the driveway, she could see P.J. waiting on the front step. Jumping up, he called out to his father and ran toward his mom's car. "They're here! They're here!" Soon, Mr. Kennedy came hurrying out of the house. It was obvious how excited P.J. was about seeing Jeremiah again. He barely gave his mother time to idle the engine before he snatched open the car door and began calling for Jeremiah to come out. When he opened his eyes, Jeremiah was just as pleased to see P.J. "C'mon," he told Jeremiah, let's play football!"

Jeremiah looked at Mrs. Kennedy. She could tell he was doing everything he could to keep from bolting out of his seat.

Mrs. Kennedy looked directly at P.J. "No hello for me?"

"Hi, Mom!" he said, pulling Jeremiah from the car. "Is it okay?"

"Yes, its fine with me, but when I call you two for dinner, make sure you come right away. Understand?"

"We understand!"

Jeremiah heard all he needed to hear. He jumped out of his seat and charged right behind P.J. They passed by Mr. Kennedy with what seemed like the speed of lighting. "Hi, Mr. Kennedy!" Jeremiah yelled as he raced with P.J. to the backyard. He had forgotten that P.J. walked with a slight limp but was amazed that when he ran, it was as though he had no limp at all.

"Hi, Jeremiah!" Mr. Kennedy called back as he greeted his wife and smiled.

"Thank you for understanding," she said.

"It's all right. We really like Jeremiah. He's a good kid. He's just had some tough breaks."

"We're having pancakes you know." Mrs. Kennedy informed her husband with a smile.

"As long as you make 'em big and golden brown the way we men like 'em." He chuckled.

Mrs. Kennedy smiled and realized how blessed she was to have a husband who was so kind and understanding. As a boy, Mr. Kennedy himself had spent many years moving from one relative's home to another after he lost his parents in a terrible car accident. If anyone knew how Jeremiah felt about being passed from home to home, it was Paul Kennedy.

He took Jeremiah's suitcase out of the trunk and carried it into the house as he walked behind his wife. "Guess we'd better get started on those pancakes!"

Jeremiah and P.J. raced all around the huge backyard playing tag. They agreed the nine-year-old maple tree that sat right in the middle of the backyard would be home base. Jeremiah could run just a little faster than P.J. and charged with all his might toward the tree.

"I'm safe!" he declared. Jeremiah studied the tree carefully. "Why's this tree so short?"

"We're growin' together," P.J. told him. "That's what my dad says."

Jeremiah had an inquisitive look on his face. "Whatta you mean?"

"My parents planted it when I was born. My dad says it's a reminder for me to keep my feet firmly planted on the ground. I don't know what that means, but he said as I grow I'll understand."

Jeremiah didn't exactly understand either, but he liked the idea of a person having his very own tree. For P.J. it was a reminder that he was growing. For Jeremiah, having a tree would say he belonged somewhere.

P.J. didn't want to talk about the tree anymore; he wanted to play. "Okay," he shouted, "let's play something else. Here," he said, tossing his football to Jeremiah, "How about tackle!"

Jeremiah missed the catch because he stood silently staring at the tree. He put his hand way down into the right pocket of his pants again and let his fingers gently reach for the paper that contained his little mustard seeds.

"What's wrong?" P.J. asked.

For a moment, Jeremiah seemed unaware that P.J. was standing there. Suddenly, all he could hear was the voice of the ol' preacher, Rev. Tatum, from his grandma's church sharing with the congregation a sermon about sowing seeds. It was hard to completely understand what he was saying about a person "reaping what they'd sown." But getting those special seeds into the ground made a whole lot of sense. The time had come for Jeremiah Jones to do some sowing of his own. And if the words of the ol' preacher were true, some reaping was sure to follow. Very carefully, he opened the paper and poured the tiny seeds into his hand. While holding them, he imagined something great someday growing out of the ground. This really was the place in his heart that he wanted to be. So he hoped the Lord might fulfill his desire for a family to call his own. Once again, he could hear Grandma Joanie encouraging him to have faith. *This is the right time*, he thought. *This is the time and the place to plant.*

P.J. came running over to Jeremiah to see what he was doing. "Whatcha got in your hand?"

Instead of answering, Jeremiah moved closer to give P.J. a better look at his treasure. Carefully, he steadied his hand to make sure not one of the special seeds fell to the ground. "Wow!" his friend said. "What are they?"

Jeremiah enthusiastically replied. "They're mustard seeds, and I need to plant them. Can I?"

"Yeah, but what do they do?"

"I'm not really sure, but I believe if I plant them, something good's gonna happen."

"Then let's do it. I'll get what we need."

P.J. ran over to the old tool shed in the far corner of the yard. When he returned, he had a trowel and a small can he'd filled with water. "You'll need these," he said, handing them to Jeremiah. "If you're gonna plant something and you want it to grow, you're gonna have to water it."

"Will you water them when I leave?"

P.J. felt good knowing that Jeremiah trusted him to look after such an important treasure. "Of course," he said without any hesitation. "I'll water 'em every day."

"And you won't forget?"

"I won't forget. Every day. I promise."

"And you won't tell nobody?"

"No . . . nobody."

The boys gave one another a firm handshake to close the deal on the secret pact they'd made, and Jeremiah began digging a small place in the earth to plant the mustard seeds. "That's good," P.J. told him, when the hole he'd dug looked just right for welcoming the seeds. Jeremiah agreed and poured a little water into the ground. Then he gently placed the seeds and covered them with the soil he'd left to the side.

"Perfect!" Jeremiah said patting down the soft soil to make it flat.

P.J. was quick to return the trowel and watering can to the shed. As soon as he closed the door, Mrs. Kennedy appeared at the kitchen window. "You boys need to come in now and clean up! Dinner will be ready soon."

Jeremiah looked at P.J., and P.J. looked at Jeremiah. At exactly the same time they both yelled loudly as they raced toward the house, "PANCAKES!"

Chapter 4

THE PRAYER

BOTH JEREMIAH AND P.J. enjoyed Mrs. Kennedy's pancakes so much that they volunteered to help clean up the kitchen. Mr. Kennedy washed the dishes while the boys each dried. Mrs. Kennedy sat down in the living room and began reading a book. Jeremiah laid his towel on the counter and peeked around the doorway. "You like to read?"

"Yes, Jeremiah, I love reading. I just don't get the chance to do it very often."

"Whatcha reading about?"

"It's a story that takes place forty years ago in an African country called Ghana."

"I like stories. Any kids in it?"

"Only two so far." She rested the book on her lap. "What kind of stories do you like?"

Jeremiah waited before answering her question. He thought very hard and suddenly he exclaimed, "I like stories about horses! They can run real fast, ya know! Got any horses in that book about Ghana?"

"No, but I'm pretty sure P.J. has a book or two about horses that he can share with you."

Jeremiah didn't see P.J. standing behind him. "I'll share, soon as you come back and do your part of the dishes," he groaned.

Jeremiah smiled and followed P.J. back to the kitchen where they noisily finished drying the dishes. It was even okay to make noise at the Kennedy house. No one yelled the words *"Be quiet."*

When the boys were done, the two of them raced upstairs to P.J.'s room to find those books about horses. There was a small bookshelf in the corner, and every one of its four shelves was filled with books. "Here it is!" P.J. called. "This is the best book about horses there is," he said handing it to Jeremiah. "You can read it before we go to bed if you want. And just like last time, you can sleep in my bed, and I'll take the sleeping bag."

"Cool! Thanks, P.J."

"You're welcome."

Jeremiah brushed his hand gently across the outside of the book and let his fingers trace around the outline of the beautiful brown horse pictured on its cover. He softly read the title and slowly tried to pronounce the author's last name. *"He Also Ran,* by Ann D a- Dan- c a r."

"It's Danacar," P.J. shouted. "Like the name Dan and a car . . . Dan-a-car!"

"What's it about?" Jeremiah inquired.

"It's about this horse that runs in a whole lotta races but never comes in first."

"Does he quit?"

"No."

"An' he never comes in first?"

"You mean does he get a blue ribbon?"

"Yeah . . . does he?"

"No, but he tries so hard that soon people come just to see him run. My dad said he really does win in the end."

"How does he win? You said he didn't get a ribbon."

"That's what *I* said, but Dad says he was a winner just because he never gave up."

Flipping through the pages Jeremiah's eyes gleamed as he looked at the pictures. "I guess . . ."

P.J. could tell many of the words were too hard for Jeremiah. "You think maybe your dad will read it to me sometime?" Jeremiah asked.

"Yeah, I think so. It's kinda hard for me too."

Jeremiah was glad P.J. understood. He sat down on the floor beside him, and the two of them looked at the pictures of the horses in the book until it was time for bed.

Just as he had promised, P.J. pulled out his sleeping bag and unfolded it on the floor.

Jeremiah could easily sleep in P.J.'s bed. It had a real nice comfortable feel. When he climbed into bed, he let himself sink down into the middle of the soft mattress. After lots of talking and giggling, the boys soon found themselves getting sleepy.

Just then, Mr. and Mrs. Kennedy walked into P.J.'s room.

"Well, boys you all seem to be having lots of fun," Mr. Kennedy said. Both P.J. and Jeremiah agreed that they were enjoying hanging out together.

"Dad, I was wondering when you and Mom were going to come to my room," P.J. said, grinning.

"We just wanted to give you guys some extra time to catch up with each other," Mrs. Kennedy added.

Recognizing why his parents had come, P.J. jumped up and grabbed Jeremiah by his hand pulling him out of the bed. The Kennedy family and Jeremiah circled up for prayer.

Mr. Kennedy led the prayer. "Dear Lord, thank You for this day and for the privilege of calling You Father. We are glad to be Your children. Thank You for loving and caring for us even when we have been disobedient and didn't deserve Your mercy. I especially thank You for my wife and son and for our special guest, Jeremiah. We are grateful that he is in our home and pray that he feels Your love demonstrated through us. Please keep us safe as we sleep tonight. It's in Jesus' Name that we pray. Amen."

Everyone said their good nights as P.J.'s parents left the room.

Jeremiah thought, *That was just like praying with Grandma Joanie.* He especially liked the part of the prayer that mentioned disobedience. He wasn't sure if he knew what mercy meant, but he understood that God still loved him even if he didn't always do what was right.

Later that night Jeremiah tossed and turned as he tried to sleep. He kept thinking that soon his time with the Kennedy family would end, and he feared he'd be on his way to a new foster home. Maybe that was the reason he ran. Maybe this was the only way he knew how to get away from his thoughts of not belonging. Jeremiah was convinced that as long as he kept moving, no one could hurt him by reminding him he was alone.

Without making a sound, he climbed out of bed and carefully stepped across P.J., who was peacefully asleep in his sleeping bag. Jeremiah walked over to the window and peered out at the blackened night sky. Looking out into the backyard, he could see only the shadow of the tree where he'd planted his seeds earlier that day. Grasping the bottom of the window, he cautiously opened it. Inhaling the cool night air, he let it fill his nostrils and lungs while he closed his eyes and placed the palms of his hands together tightly to make sure the prayer he was about to say would be answered. "I want to stay here more than anything I ever wanted . . . even more than the dark blue mountain bike. I like this family, and I think they like me. If you can hear me, God, please let me stay. Amen."

Jeremiah thought of another one of Grandma Joanie's *"strong words."* "Expectation," she'd say, "can make all the difference in the world when it comes to something happening or not. Expect it, believe it, and wait for it."

In the silence of the night, Jeremiah opened his eyes, unfolded his hands, and once again looked out into the sky. He stared, and he waited. Just as he was about to return to bed, he witnessed a beautiful gleaming star as it sped across the sky. "I see it!" he whispered excitedly. "I see it!" In what seemed like a microsecond, Jeremiah believed that the tiny star of magnificent brilliance had been a message sent to him. He was sure that it was. Gently, he closed the window, smiled, tiptoed across the room, and crawled back into bed. Resting on his back, he gazed up at the ceiling. He could see himself living with the Kennedys for the rest of his life and wondered if they could see him as part of their family as well. Again, he remembered the first time he'd stayed with them, how Mr. Kennedy had played football with him and P.J. in the backyard. After catching the ball, he could hear Mr. Kennedy yelling, "Run, Jeremiah run! Run as fast as you can! You can do it! Make a touchdown!" But instead he stopped in his tracks and looked at Mr. Kennedy with a puzzled expression. As far back as Jeremiah could recall that was the first and only time in his young life he wasn't being scolded for running. "It's okay," Mr. Kennedy assured him. "It's okay."

In that moment Jeremiah could hear reassurance in Mr. Kennedy's voice and was able to breathe a sigh of relief feeling at ease. He was more comfortable there than anywhere else he could remember since losing Grandma Joanie. The Kennedy home wasn't the same as his grandma's, yet the warmth he felt when he stepped across the threshold of their front door leading to the inside was very similar. There were always lots of laughter and enough hugs to go around for everyone.

There was no doubt in his mind or in his heart. He knew this was the one place in the world he wanted to be. "If I don't make any mistakes, I'll be all right," he said encouraging himself. "And if they let me stay, I won't run. I'll be good every day." His eyes widened the same way they used to at Christmas time. "Expectation," he repeated, rolling over on his side. "Expect it, believe it, and wait for it." He could hear Grandma Joanie's sweet voice whispering to him just as she had done so many times before, "It's gonna be all right Jeremiah . . . it's gonna be all right."

Jeremiah picked up the book about horses and struggled with the words in it, but he wouldn't allow himself to fall asleep until he had pretended to read every page. He studied the pictures and quietly spoke words that he thought matched them.

When he was done, he carefully placed the book under his pillow and finally could feel himself drifting off to sleep. *"He Also Ran,"* he said brushing his hand over the title. "I thought I was the only one who did that."

Chapter (5)

SATURDAY MORNING

SATURDAY MORNING CAME faster than Jeremiah expected. From the time his head touched the pillow it seemed only minutes had passed. He tried to roll over and pull the warm, cozy comforter over his head when he felt someone rustling the covers. "C'mon, Jeremiah, get up!" It was P.J. trying to roust him out of bed.

"I wanna sleep," Jeremiah whined, while he buried himself deeper under the blanket.

"But I'm gonna race today! It's a track meet, and my dad is taking us. I want you to see me run!"

Jeremiah instantly threw back the covers and bombarded P.J. with tons of questions. "Run? You run? Where do you run? I never seen you runnin' nowhere."

"At the park there's a track. My dad coaches us, and I want you to come! Look, I got a uniform and everything."

P.J. beamed. He was so proud of his uniform and stood strong and proud as he spoke.

Jeremiah gazed at the bright gold T-shirt and royal blue shorts P.J. was wearing. "That ain't no real uniform," he said. His words pierced P.J. like a pointed dart that had reached its bull's-eye. As soon as he had spoken those words, Jeremiah wanted to pick them up and put them back into his mouth, but he knew the damage had already been done. He could see how hurtful his comment was to P.J., and the last thing he wanted to do was to hurt someone who had only tried to befriend him. If only P.J. could read his mind, he thought. Then he would know what Jeremiah was really feeling in his heart. Secretly, he wished he were wearing a bright gold T-shirt and a pair of royal blue shorts, too. "I'm sorry," he said getting out of bed. "I didn't mean it . . . I—"

"It's okay," P.J. said waving his hand. "It's just that our team really ain't so good, but I wanted you to come an' see us anyway. It feels good to have somebody cheering for us, even though we probably won't win."

Jeremiah agreed with what P.J. was saying about hearing people cheer for you. He felt wonderful every time he heard Grandma Joanie encouraging him to do his best and to keep trying harder. She would hug him when he had a good day in school, and she would hug him when he didn't. "Hugs are free," she'd say and then give him another one. It was as though she was storing up those hugs so Jeremiah could keep their memory safely stored in his heart. Grandma Joanie had been his very own cheering section, so surely he was familiar with that good feeling P.J. was talking about. He missed the cheers and the hugs so much that sometimes it hurt just to try and remember them.

Jeremiah reached under the pillow and pulled out the book they had taken from P.J.'s shelf the night before. "Can I bring it?" he asked, as he held the book carefully in two hands and stared at the picture of the beautiful chestnut brown stallion on the cover.

P.J. could see the eagerness in Jeremiah's eyes. "Yeah, but you better c'mon."

Jeremiah hurried to get himself dressed and followed P.J. downstairs so they could have breakfast. "Think we'll have pancakes again?" he asked.

"I don't think so," P.J. told him. "It'll probably be cereal."

"How do you know?"

" 'Cause my dad's making breakfast," he said grinning.

Just as they were about to leave the room, Jeremiah ran over to the bed and grabbed P.J.'s book about horses. "Don't want to forget this!" he said holding the book up high.

P.J. warned him. "Just don't let nothing happen to it."

"I won't," Jeremiah said, carefully tucking the book under his arm as though he was securing a great treasure. "Thanks!"

"Sure, but we need to get downstairs *now*!"

"What's the rush?"

"My dad will think we don't like his cooking," P.J. said laughing.

By the time the boys got downstairs and entered the kitchen, Mr. Kennedy was putting the bowls on the table. He opened the door of a narrow pantry and reached for a big box of cereal called "Crunchos" and began pouring some into each bowl. "I hope you like this kind, Jeremiah. P.J. says it's the best because it's got lots of crunch to it."

Mr. Kennedy didn't have to say anything. P.J. was a true-to-life commercial for the company. The second he sat down in his seat, he grabbed the milk, poured it on his cereal, and began heaping spoonfuls of "Crunchos" into his mouth.

"Ah hum!" Mr. Kennedy said, clearing his throat. He looked at his son and waited for a response. When he didn't get one, he decided to intervene. "Did we forget something, son?"

Jeremiah still sat with his bowl piled high with "Crunchos," waiting for some kind of signal that would let him know it was okay to begin eating. P.J. put down his spoon, closed his eyes, and folded his hands. Jeremiah folded his hands and closed his eyes, too.

"Thank You, Lord, for this food and that it tastes so good . . . oh, and thank You for Jeremiah comin' to stay with us. And could you please help us win today? Amen."

"Amen," Jeremiah repeated.

"You boys need to finish quickly so we can go. The meet starts at eleven, and we want to be there on time. You know what happens when you don't show up on time?" Jeremiah shook his head *no*, while P.J. shook his head *yes*. Mr. Kennedy answered. "Disqualified. That's one thing we don't want. We may not win, but we want our chance to run. Eat up, Jeremiah," he said. "You're coming with us."

Jeremiah was happy to hear that Mr. Kennedy wanted him to come along. He started to eat so fast he felt as if he might pop like a balloon. Within a few minutes, his cereal was gone, and he quickly picked up his bowl and gulped down the leftover milk. "Wow!" P.J. exclaimed. "I never saw nobody eat and drink that fast!"

When Mr. Kennedy saw how quickly Jeremiah had finished his breakfast, he tried to set his mind at ease. "Jeremiah, we want to be on time, but you didn't have to eat so fast. It's not good for your digestion when you rush like that."

"Sorry," Jeremiah said, hanging his head. He felt he had made his second mistake at the Kennedy breakfast table and knew he could not afford to make any more. P.J. had been nice enough to forgive him when he made fun of his uniform, and now this. *Why can't I just do what is right?* he asked himself. He needed to be perfect; so perfect that the Kennedys would want to keep him forever. He reminded himself to guard his tongue and his behavior. This was one time he knew he couldn't afford to "mess up." And if he had any power at all, he would use every ounce of it to do all the right things that would make Mr. and Mrs. Kennedy and P.J. realize that he was the missing piece of their family puzzle. In his mind, Jeremiah believed he had come there to make that puzzle complete.

Jeremiah waited until P.J. finished his breakfast, and when he got up to put his bowl and spoon in the sink, he did exactly the same. He looked over at Mr. Kennedy, who was finishing his morning coffee and said, "Is Mrs. Kennedy coming with us?"

"No, she had some errands to run early this morning, though I'm hoping she'll get back in time to see the race."

Jeremiah hoped she would get back in time, too. He figured she was probably one of the loudest voices cheering from the stands as she watched her son run around the track hoping for a victory.

P.J. turned on the water and added liquid detergent. He looked around to make sure his dad wasn't watching. And when he saw him leave the room, he stuck both hands into the bubbling water and scooped up two handfuls of fluffy soapsuds. Jeremiah wanted more than anything to stick his hands in, too, but a little voice inside said *no*. He knew he wanted to reach in and scoop up his own foaming mountain and blow it back into the sink, but he convinced himself it wasn't worth the risk. He could wait until he was a member of the family. Then, just like P.J., he could play in the soapy water and know his place in the Kennedy home would always be secure.

P.J. washed the bowls and pointed to a dishtowel hanging on the wall. "You dry, and then we'll be done."

Jeremiah did as he was told. He reached for the dishtowel and began drying the bowls and spoons as P.J. placed them in the dish drainer. Suddenly, they could hear the sound of a car horn blaring from outside. P.J. knew it was his dad summoning them to get in the car. It was time to go, so Jeremiah quickly dried the last spoon, neatly folded the towel and returned it to its proper place. "I think we're gonna win today," P.J. said confidently.

"How do you know?" Jeremiah asked.

"I dunno," P.J. said with a smile.

As the boys left the kitchen and headed out to the car, P.J. gave Jeremiah a pat on the back. "It's gonna be different today," he said wearing a great big grin.

Jeremiah smiled back, and with all the enthusiasm he could muster, he said, "Yeah, I hope we win!"

BOYS 'N BLUE

JEREMIAH SAT in the backseat of Mr. Kennedy's car while P.J. sat in front, busily talking to his father about the upcoming track meet. As much as he wanted to, Jeremiah was careful not to jump into the conversation. Still, he didn't allow his silence to keep him from imagining himself positioned at the starting line of the tar covered track. He pictured himself anxiously waiting in his own lane, a lane that was distinctly separated from the others by freshly painted white lines. He smiled as he stared out the window, looking beyond the pretty tree lined streets that soon led directly up the drive to the Cooper Middle School Athletic Field. When they arrived, Jeremiah sat up and looked with amazement at all the children who had gathered on this morning "just to run."

"Hurry, Dad," P.J. urged his father. "Like you said, we don't want to be late!" In his excitement, P.J. noticed two of the boys from his team just about to enter the field. "Hey,

Ronnie! Hey, Mike!" he yelled sticking his head out of the window. "Wait up!"

As soon as Mr. Kennedy parked the car, P.J. and Jeremiah jumped out. "C'mon, Jeremiah," he said, while the two tried to catch up with P.J.'s friends. Jeremiah very quickly remembered the promise he'd made to himself about not making any mistakes. He stopped in his tracks and turned around to face Mr. Kennedy. "It's okay, Jeremiah. You can go," he said. "Make sure you stay with P.J. I'll be right there."

Right away, Jeremiah took off to catch up with P.J. "Thanks, Mr. Kennedy!" he yelled, waving as he looked back. "P.J.!" he called out. "Wait for me!" By the time he caught up to the others, they had just about reached the track. P.J. sat down on the bleachers talking with Mike and Ronnie. And soon Jeremiah found himself standing right in front of the three boys. "Man, you're fast!" P.J. told him. "You got over here real quick."

Mike was the shortest runner on the team, but he was also one of the fastest. He looked younger than ten and got angry whenever anyone made the mistake of thinking he was eight. He folded his arms across his chest and gave Jeremiah a look that seemed to study him from head to toe. "Who's this?" he asked.

P.J. stepped down to where Jeremiah was standing and pulled him close. "This is Jeremiah. He's staying with us."

"He's your cousin?" Ronnie asked.

"No, he's a friend."

Mike stood up looking very serious. "Can he run?"

"I dunno about running in a meet," P.J. said, putting the attention on Jeremiah. "But he got over here real quick!"

"Can you run?" Mike demanded.

For the first time since he had come to stay with the Kennedys, Jeremiah appeared confident. "Can I run? I bet I'm probably the best runner you ever saw."

"Aww, I bet you can't run at all," Mike said, waving his hand.

Ronnie decided to add in his "two cents." "Well," he said, "if George don't show up, I think we should let Jeremiah run with our team."

George, whom Ronnie referred to, was none other than George Radcliff Jr., the team's self-appointed captain. Since his dad was in charge of scheduling all the teams, young George somehow felt that gave him the authority to make decisions as well.

Just then the boys saw Mr. Kennedy approaching the bleachers and ran over to him. "Hey, Mr. Kennedy," Mike said. "Like my new sneakers? My dad said they're the best. I just know I'll run faster today. You watch and see."

Mr. Kennedy pushed back his cap as though making sure he got a clear look at Mike's new sneakers. "Yeah," he said, "they're the real thing all right. And you know what? You probably *will* run faster today."

"Thanks, Mr. Kennedy. I'm really gonna try."

Now it was Jeremiah's turn to look. He stared at Mike's new sneakers and found himself agreeing with the boy who was so outspoken. Mike was right. From what Jeremiah saw, they were probably the best sneakers in the whole world. Jeremiah had never seen anything like them. Even the laces were special. He thought about how he too could probably run faster if he had a pair just like them.

Mr. Kennedy looked over at P.J. "Did everybody meet Jeremiah?"

"Yes," P.J. replied. "They even want him to run with us today."

"I didn't say nothing about him running with us," Mike said. "That was Ronnie."

Mike pointed at Jeremiah. "He said if George don't come, maybe he could run with us."

Ronnie quickly denied everything Mike said. "I did not!" he shouted.

"Yes, you did," Mike said moving toward him.

Mr. Kennedy stepped in between the two of them and put an end to what looked like the makings of an argument. "I'm sure George will be here soon. He hasn't missed a meet yet, and I don't think he'll miss today's. Besides, Jeremiah wouldn't be able to sub because he's not officially on the team."

"Nobody would know." Ronnie snickered.

"They'd know," Mike argued. "He's wearin' regular clothes. I think *everybody* would notice that! Plus, he's wearin' shoes. We'd all get dis . . . dis . . ."

"Disqualified," P.J. declared. "We'd get kicked out of the race."

"I don't want that to happen," Mike declared.

In that moment, Jeremiah learned something about Mike. He may have been one to "talk big" and make a lot of noise, but when it came down to it, he wanted to do things the right way. Jeremiah remembered Mr. Kennedy saying at breakfast that being disqualified wasn't a good thing. And he was absolutely certain it didn't have anything to do with winning. He could tell by the way everyone's expression changed as soon as P.J. said the word that this was something he couldn't do. He would have loved a chance to run with team, but if it was going to end with the others getting mad at him, he wanted no part of it. Just then, P.J. spotted someone getting out of a car on the far side of the field. It was George Radcliff, so there was no further need to discuss the possibility of Jeremiah running with the track team today.

George came running to where the rest of the team had assembled. He didn't look very much like a runner at all. By the time he reached the other boys, he was puffing as if he was out of breath. His bright red hair was dripping with pellets of sweat that rolled down his forehead, skidded past his freckles, and was scooped up with his hand before they could go any farther. "Hi, Mr. Kennedy! How's our team today?"

Everyone knew George was the real reason for their losing streak because he never finished. Usually, half way around his leg of the race, he'd stop. No matter how much his teammates cheered for him to keep going, he always failed to cross the finish line.

"Doing good, George," Mr. Kennedy answered. "We're all doing good."

Ronnie whispered in Mike's ear. "When did we become *his* team?"

"I wouldn't talk too loud," Mike warned. "Remember, his dad bought us these uniforms."

"You're right . . . we don't have any trophies, but we *do* have uniforms." Ronnie looked over at George and shook his head as though annoyed. He wondered why out of all the track teams in their division George had to pick theirs. Ronnie felt they were never going to win. It didn't matter whether they put George in the first position, somewhere in the middle, or at the end. George Radcliff wasn't only the heaviest boy in the league, he was the slowest, too.

Jeremiah stood gazing out at the track. He could see himself running all the way around it and maybe even going around it again, if only he could get the chance. Nothing seemed more fun than the idea of being able to run and not get into trouble or yelled at for doing it.

While a number of the other teams had begun to gather at the starting area, many of the runners were doing their stretching exercises, and Mr. Kennedy informed his team that they needed to begin stretching as well. Jeremiah knew he couldn't run with P.J.'s team, but nobody told him he couldn't stretch with them.

"Whatcha doin'?" George asked him. Jeremiah pointed at the other boys on the team.

"I'm doin' what they're doin.' I'm stretchin.'" It was very obvious that Jeremiah wanted to be a runner, too.

"What are you stretchin' for if you ain't runnin'?"

Jeremiah thought about George's question and wondered the same thing. Why was he stretching like the other boys? He wasn't going to run with them no matter how much he wanted to. *Maybe I should just sit down on the bleachers and wait,* he thought. But he decided if he couldn't be in the race, he'd settle for doing the warm-up exercises with them. It felt good just pretending to be part of the team. So he kept bending and stretching until Mr. Kennedy blew his whistle signaling for them to stop. When he did this, all the boys hustled over to where he was standing.

"How many races are there?" Jeremiah asked P.J.

"A whole lot, but we're only gonna be in the team relay today."

"That's the one I like the best," Jeremiah said smiling; though secretly he had no idea what a team relay was. "You gotta name?" he asked.

P.J. laughed at Jeremiah's question. "You know my name; it's P.J."

Jeremiah shook his head. "No, I mean the team. What is it?"

Mike interrupted and pointed at his shirt. "See the color?" he said, putting himself between P.J. and Jeremiah. "It's blue! We're the *Blue Team*." Then he pointed at another group of boys. "See them over there? Their shirts are red. That makes them the *Red Team*."

"Oh," said Jeremiah. He decided it was time to stop asking questions. Mr. Kennedy blew his whistle again to get everyone's attention. "Jeremiah," he called out while pointing at the bleachers, "you can sit right there. Mrs. Kennedy will be here soon. You'll be able to see the race real good from there."

Jeremiah walked over to the bleachers, climbed to the fourth row, and sat down. In a matter of a few minutes, he found himself surrounded by parents, grandparents, and brothers and sisters of the runners assembled that day for the big race. They had taken their seats in the bleachers, and Jeremiah knew it must have been getting close to the time for the races to begin. He turned around and searched the parking lot for as far as his eyes could see, wondering when Mrs. Kennedy would arrive. The excitement he felt coming from those around him gave the Saturday race an Olympic-type feel. To the right of the bleachers he saw a long table. On it were blue, red, and yellow ribbons. Jeremiah knew these ribbons would be awarded to the runners who would take first, second, and third place in the day's events. He wished he had brought the book from Mr. Kennedy's car. Then he could look at the pictures of the beautiful horse again. Instead, he dared to dream of being one of the runners and imagined himself zooming around the track with the speed of lightning. He carefully watched every move of the day's competitors, who all stood like champions ready to break new records.

The runners racing in the 400 meter relay were getting themselves ready at the starting line. Jeremiah looked up and saw Mrs. Kennedy hustling toward the bleachers. She yelled out and waved to P.J., who was the second runner on his team. He looked a little embarrassed but at the same time seemed relieved that his mom had made it in time to see him run. George also studied the faces in the stands, hoping to see his dad. But he didn't, and it made him wonder why he hadn't come. He would be the third runner for the team today, so there was still a chance maybe his dad would get there before the end of the race.

"Mrs. Kennedy! Over here!" Jeremiah yelled, pointing at the empty space right next to him.

"Whew!" she said, making her way up to the fourth row where Jeremiah had positioned himself to get the best possible view. "I was afraid I was going to miss the race."

"I think they're gonna start now, Mrs. Kennedy!" he shouted.

Jeremiah smiled and silently thanked God that Mrs. Kennedy had made it in time.

Chapter 7

THE MEET

SUDDENLY THE SOUND of the announcer's voice could be heard over the entire field. *"On your mark! Get set! Go!"* The starting pistol was fired, and from that second, Jeremiah's attention was focused on the runners as they sped around the track. Each one was careful to stay in his own lane.

For this event, a baton was passed to each runner as he started his part of the course. P.J.'s team was competing against five other teams comprised of runners ages nine and ten. The only thing distinguishing one team from the other was the color of the T-shirts worn for the day's competition.

Mike was designated as the lead runner for the Blue Team, and at the sound of the starting pistol he charged off from the starting line with all of his might. He could feel himself running against the wind as it gently whipped against the sides of his face. His left hand held tightly on to the baton as he used it to propel himself through the air to finish his leg of the race.

P.J. was next, so he waited for Mike to get as close to him as he could. When the time was right, P.J. reached his hand out to grasp the baton. He was more than ready. He knew speed was important, but if the handoff wasn't complete, it could ruin the entire run. He focused himself just as his dad had taught him to do. As soon as he could feel the baton in his hand, he tightly clasped his fingers around it and darted off to run the second leg of the race. He could hear the sound of voices yelling, "Go, P.J.! You can do it! All the way! All the way!" It was Mr. and Mrs. Kennedy, Jeremiah, and the rest of his teammates. Their cheers and excitement seemed to give him extra energy as he made his way around the track. He felt he was moving faster, and when he saw that he had just about reached the end of his portion of the run, he leaned forward with the baton to give himself a little more of an edge. He could see George's hand held out and waiting for him to come and hand off the baton.

The palm of George's left hand was perspiring uncontrollably, and he began to worry that something might go wrong. George was the third runner for the team, so the minute he stepped off, everyone knew the Blue Team had made it halfway through the race. George smiled the second he could feel the smooth wooden stick resting in the palm of his hand. He wanted his feet to move faster but was pleased enough just knowing the baton was still in his hand. He could see Ronnie waiting up ahead when the worst thing that could happen, did happen. George dropped the baton. And when he turned around to pick it up, he found that he was encircled by the wind created by the rest of the runners as they speedily passed by him. Ronnie yelled as loudly as he could. "C'mon, George! Keep goin'!"

George could feel himself breathing harder, and his brain was telling his legs to move, but just as in times past, the rest of him had decided to give up. He stood there silently watching as each of the other runners passed their batons to the last runner on their team. Though his teammates were still yelling his name, he could no longer hear them. He bent down, picked up the baton, and walked the rest of his leg of the race. Finally, he could see Ronnie waiting up ahead still positioning himself to get ready for the handoff of the baton. The sound of his teammates yelling got louder. "C'mon, George! Run!" Holding the baton in the crevice of his left arm, he cupped his hands over his ears to block out the sound of their voices.

George had once again given up, and when he passed the baton to Ronnie, the other teams were so far ahead, it didn't matter. The Blue Team knew they were on their way to losing another race. And once again, they could deposit their loss directly into the lap of George Radcliff. Ronnie saw the last runner for the Red Team cross the finish line and knew for a fact there was no possible chance of winning. But when George finally reached him, he grabbed the baton and ran his distance with the same force and power he would have used had he been in first place instead of last. Ronnie ran alone, and he could see the finish line up ahead and crossed it.

With his head hanging down, George stood silently waiting with the rest of the team. He wanted to apologize but didn't know what to say. He had already said he was sorry after causing the team to lose the last five races. After a while, he knew these were words no one wanted to hear. And he sensed his team-mates had probably stopped listening to him more than a few races ago. Like the others on the team, he was tired of losing, and beyond that, he was tired of being the cause of all their losses.

"We were in the lead!" Mike yelled. Disappointment was written all over his face, and though he tried to hide it, and would certainly never admit it, he was crying.

"Yeah," Ronnie shouted, "we shoulda won!"

Mike was fuming. He gritted his teeth and looked squarely at George. "And we woulda if it wasn't for—"

"Me," George said finishing Mike's sentence. "It was me." Again he stood silent with his head lowered. Clearly he was ashamed and embarrassed about doing so poorly in the race yet again.

Mr. Kennedy walked over to where his team was standing and interrupted. "You all did great out there today!" He patted George on the back. "And I could see you're trying to work on your speed."

Mike nudged P.J. in the arm and whispered. "Speed? What speed? He doesn't have any."

P.J. gave a half smile to Mike's comment.

Ronnie stepped forward and glanced over at George. "Some of us did try, Mr. Kennedy, but when are we ever gonna win? I'm sick of losing all the time."

"Me too," Mike agreed.

P.J.'s eyes turned toward his dad. He didn't say anything, but the sadness in his eyes told the same story. He was tired of losing too. He knew his dad would say something the team needed to hear. He always did. Somehow, even though they had never won a blue, a red, or even a yellow ribbon, Mr. Kennedy could always find just the right words to make the team feel as if they at least had a chance. It wasn't unusual for him to load up the team into the car and take them out for "victory ice cream." And if one of the boys reminded him that they hadn't won, he'd simply say they were celebrating the victory which was to come. P.J. wasn't so sure about his teammates, but he believed what his father told them and in his mind created a picture of the day when the Blue Team would hold out their hands and receive their winning ribbons. But for today, the pain they all were feeling from today's loss was still very real.

Just as the other teams were coming off the field, one boy from the Green Team, the team that had taken third place in the relay, tapped George on the arm as they walked by. "Thanks, man," he said wearing a smirk on his face. "Couldna done it without ya."

"All right, team," Mr. Kennedy called out. "Let's do it!"

This was the part Mike hated the most. Whether win or lose, Mr. Kennedy never forgot to have his team shake hands with their opponents. And as always, they put themselves in the same line order in which they ran and shook the hands of the winners.

"Now that wasn't so bad, was it?" Mr. Kennedy asked.

Mrs. Kennedy and Jeremiah came down from the bleachers and greeted the team. "You're all running much better," Mrs. Kennedy encouraged. "You looked real good out there today."

Jeremiah excitedly stuck his head into the group. "An' it was the best race I ever saw in my whole life."

"How many races you seen?" Ronnie asked.

Jeremiah thought for a moment. "One, but if I had seen

some more, this still woulda been the best."

Mr. Kennedy could see that his team was more than a little down about losing another race. "How about we go and have some ice cream? We can go over to Fifty Plus Flavors."

No matter how bad George may have been feeling, he quickly took the bait. "I'm in, Mr. Kennedy!" he yelled.

Ronnie took his foot and kicked up some dirt. "I don't want no more ice cream. I'm sick of ice cream. I wanna win a race!"

Mrs. Kennedy could tell that maybe her husband's system of reward had possibly run its course. It appeared the boys were tired of getting treats when they hadn't done anything to earn them. "I don't think Coach Kennedy feels good about losing either," she said. "Maybe having some ice cream will help *him* feel better." She glanced over at her husband and saw him smile. It was easy to see that the two of them also worked as a team of their own. Her words were pretty convincing, because, when the boys looked at Mr. Kennedy, they resolved they could have at least one more ice cream "for him."

"I guess I'll go," Ronnie said, as he used his foot to smooth over the dirt he had kicked.

"Me too," Mike added.

"I don't have a choice," P.J. chuckled. "And if I did, I'd choose a double scoop of chocolate with lots of nuts and some whipped cream on top."

Jeremiah, who had been quiet up to that point, stepped forward and looked directly into Mr. Kennedy's eyes. He studied them and thought about how Grandma Joanie always told him how you can see a "whole lot when you look somebody in the eyes. They're like a mirror," she'd say. "And a mirror don't lie."

Mr. Kennedy's eyes, Jeremiah told himself, were kind. "Can I have ice cream too?" he asked quietly.

Mr. Kennedy pointed to where the grassy area ended. "If you can beat me in a race from here to there, you can have as many scoops as you like."

P.J. screamed the count. *"One . . . Two . . . Three . . . GO!"*

Jeremiah didn't need to hear another word. In what seemed like a flash, he began running toward the end of the field carefully looking back every few seconds to make sure Mr. Kennedy didn't run past him.

"I made it!" he yelled. "I got here first, and you owe me three scoops of ice cream!"

Mr. Kennedy wasn't surprised that Jeremiah got there first, but he was amazed at how fast he did it. "Wow!" he exclaimed. "Look at that kid go!"

When Mr. and Mrs. Kennedy and the others reached the car, Mr. Kennedy reached down into his pocket and pulled out a twenty dollar bill. He held it up high so Jeremiah could see it. "I hope this will be enough. I'd be smart not to challenge you again."

Jeremiah nodded his head *yes* and climbed into Mr. Kennedy's car with P.J. and George, while Mike and Ronnie rode with Mrs. Kennedy. "You oughta be on our team," Ronnie called over to him.

Mike agreed. "Yeah, you run so fast I bet we could win if you was runnin' with us."

"Thanks," Jeremiah said. He sat back in his seat and felt good that for once in his life someone was glad he knew how to run. He wondered if it was too much to ask God, in addition to letting him stay with the Kennedys, to also find a place for him on P.J.'s track team. And he didn't care if he ever won a blue ribbon. He just wanted a chance to run with the wooden baton and pass it on to a teammate, as he had just seen the others do during the track meet. Maybe once a placement was found for him, if it was a home close by, Mr. and Mrs. Kennedy would let him run with the team sometime. Feeling a little cramped because he shared the backseat of Mr. Kennedy's car with some ever-present sports equipment and now George, Jeremiah burrowed himself in a corner and prayed real hard that by the next meet there might be a spot on the team just for him.

Chapter 8

ICE CREAM 'N DREAMS

JEREMIAH ENJOYED HIMSELF as he ate as many spoonfuls of his three-scoop banana split as he could. Holding his stomach, giving off an enormous sigh, and wearing a huge grin of satisfaction, he stated, "I'm done!"

"I knew you wasn't gonna be able to eat no three scoops," said Ronnie. "The only person I ever seen able to do that is George."

Just then everyone looked over at George who was about to finish his third scoop of vanilla, chocolate, and rocky road combination. Holding the last spoonful to his mouth, he slowly placed it back in the dish when he realized he was now the center of everyone's attention. "I'm done too," he said. "It's a tie between me and Jeremiah."

"Yep," Jeremiah agreed, "it's a tie!"

George gave Jeremiah a pat on the back and smiled. He was relieved that Jeremiah didn't seek to challenge him. He knew he didn't want any more ice cream and often ate more than the other boys because he knew he could. That, he told himself, was one contest he surely could win. George and Jeremiah shook hands and resolved they were "equal" ice cream scoop eating champions.

"I believe our work here is done," Mr. Kennedy joked. As he paid for all the ice cream his team had eaten, Mrs. Kennedy and the boys headed to the parking lot. Once again, she would drive Mike and Ronnie, while Mr. Kennedy would drive George, P.J., and Jeremiah. "See you at home," he told her as his charges got into the car.

By the time they got back home, Jeremiah and P.J. had fallen asleep in the backseat. Jeremiah was clutching the book he had borrowed from P.J. He was dreaming about what a great day it had been and the fun he'd had seeing his first track meet and being with the Kennedy family. After Mr. Kennedy pulled into the driveway, Mrs. Kennedy soon pulled up behind him. She got out of her car and opened the back door of her husband's car and gave each of the boys a little tug. "Okay, you two, we're home. I want you each to make sure you take a shower and then off to bed," she directed. "It's been a long day."

P.J. sat up, gave a great big yawn, and rubbed his eyes. "Okay, Mom." He gave Jeremiah another shake. "C'mon, Jeremiah, we're home. Get out of the car." Jeremiah moved slowly as he seemed to force his body out of the cozy nook he had created for himself in the backseat.

"Okay, okay," he said, sliding himself across the seat and out the door. As though he had been given some kind of jolt, Jeremiah remembered something very important. He stared at P.J. and said, "There's somethin' I gotta do." Jeremiah began running toward the backyard, with P.J. following, which confused Mr. and Mrs. Kennedy.

"Where are you boys going?" Mrs. Kennedy inquired.

"We'll be right back!" P.J. answered. "We promise!"

Jeremiah opened the gate, and they ran toward the red maple tree sitting in the middle of the backyard. When they reached it, Jeremiah stood quiet and shook his head. He was greatly disappointed and began crying. "It didn't work," he said staring at the ground. "It didn't work."

P.J. knew Jeremiah was referring to the mustard seeds he had planted the day before. He tried to find words that would make his friend feel better. "It takes more than a day for something to grow, Jeremiah. Look at us. It's gonna take a whole lotta years before we finish growin'."

"I know," Jeremiah said sadly, "but a day was all I had."

Without saying another word, the two boys quietly walked toward the house. Jeremiah wiped his eyes while P.J. glanced back at the area next to the tree where Jeremiah had planted his seeds and hoped for the sake of his friend that something might grow.

Jeremiah reminded himself about the wonderful day he'd had. It was a day he would always remember. Unlike the tiny mountains of ice cream scoops he had so easily devoured earlier that day, the mountain he faced of finding a permanent home was the kind only God could move. So he searched his heart for some of those *strong words* his grandma had shared with him and silently prayed that the Lord would hear his prayer and bless him with an answer. Thinking about Grandma Joanie and praying with the Kennedy family before going to bed also helped him feel better.

Jeremiah was very tired, so he wasted no time getting himself ready for bed. Facing the reality that this would probably be his last night sleeping in P.J.'s nicely decorated room made him all the more anxious to greet the comfortable feeling he got smelling the freshly laundered sheets and pillow. And he loved the way his head melted into the fluffy pillow that had been plumped to its seams with goose feathers. Jeremiah hoped this would be a long night so he could enjoy every second of P.J.'s warm cozy bed. *Maybe I'll have a great dream,* he thought. *A dream that when I wake up and look out the window, I'll see a brand new tree growing from my mustard seeds.* He said quietly to himself, "That's what I'm gonna dream tonight. I'm gonna dream about a great big tree growin' from my mustard seeds."

P.J. had already tucked himself neatly inside his sleeping bag and was almost asleep. "Huh?" he asked. "You say something?"

"Just planning my dream," Jeremiah said, grinning while he slid himself in between the comfy sheets.

P.J. started to tell him that you couldn't plan what you wanted to dream when you sleep, but he was too tired and instead put his head down and issued a warning. "Better get some sleep, Jeremiah. We gotta get up early tomorrow."

Jeremiah quickly pulled the covers back and sat up straight. "Early? But tomorrow's Sunday."

"Yeah, an' that means we're going to church at eight o'-clock."

Jeremiah's eyes widened. He hadn't been to a church service since his grandma's passing. "Eight o'clock in the morning?"

P.J. turned himself over as though trying to find just the perfect spot in his sleeping bag. "Uh-huh."

"Man!" he said. "That's kinda early. Think everybody's gonna be awake?"

"Oh yeah . . . we *all* will. Now go to sleep."

Jeremiah closed his eyes and concentrated on going to sleep. After a little while he could feel himself getting drowsy and finally drifted off. However, he didn't sleep for very long. A few hours later, a large beam of moonlight managed to sneak its way through the window and rested over him. The light's strength had awakened him. Jeremiah sat up and leaned over the side of the bed to see where the moonbeam ended. He smiled when he saw that a small part of it rested on P.J., who was peacefully sleeping on the floor. He wanted to know again what it felt like to sleep and feel that kind of peace. He wanted to wake up in the morning knowing he had a family of his own. Was that moonbeam the sign of hope he'd been waiting for?

Ever so restless, he tossed and turned over and over in bed. First he tried to rest on his right side, then on his left, but nothing seemed to work. He wished he could stop moving and just be still. He thought about how everyone at his old school wanted him to sit still. Jeremiah smiled as he wondered what they would think if they knew he was trying. Unfortunately, on this night he wasn't having any success. And even if he couldn't be still, he prayed for a family that would allow him to stay anyway. He knew there was a family like that somewhere because Grandma Joanie used to say, "God has special people in special places here on earth to love His children." For a moment, Jeremiah closed his eyes and prayed that *his* special people were the Kennedys.

Just as he could feel his eyelids getting heavy, Jeremiah suddenly thought he could hear Mr. and Mrs. Kennedy talking in the room next door. He stood up, leaned against the headboard, and pressed his ear hard against the wall, hoping he could hear what they were saying. He was sure he had heard his name mentioned but quickly covered his ears, fearing he might overhear plans of sending him on to another foster home. He remembered Grandma Joanie telling him that the good Lord had not given him ears for eavesdropping on other people's conversations. "Whatever you're supposed to know," she'd say, "God will let you know when *He's* ready."

Jeremiah knew his grandma never wasted words. What she said, she believed. And she stood by what she believed even when she didn't have a neatly tied up answer that she could point to and say, "Look, there's my proof, and that's how I know what I know." She just simply believed, and "this lesson," she told her grandson, was called "having faith." Jeremiah took joy in the lessons his grandma shared, but now with her gone, he found it very hard to have the faith she talked about. "Water-walking faith, Jeremiah," she'd tell him. "Believe what the Lord can do even when you can't see it with your eyes."

Jeremiah closed his eyes and pictured himself living his to-morrows with Mr. and Mrs. Kennedy and P.J. Satisfied with his thoughts, he would be able to sleep now. And knowing he had no vote in where he would go, he decided to hold on to Grandma Joanie's *"strong words"* as tightly as he was holding on to P.J.'s pillow. Softly, Jeremiah whispered to himself. "Whatever I'm supposed to know, God'll let me know." Laying his head down gently on the pillow, he closed his eyes, and finally drifted off to sleep.

Chapter 9

SUNDAY MORNIN'

IT WASN'T LONG before last night's moonbeam had moved aside and made way for the fresh morning's sun rays that danced their way into the room, making their presence known on every wall and corner. Jeremiah awakened to the smell of bacon and what he hoped were pancakes being prepared in the kitchen. He gave a huge yawn and the widest stretch his arms could manage. He then leaned over the side of the bed and was surprised to find that P.J. was already up. Quickly, Jeremiah jumped out of bed, opened the door, and peeked around the corner. "P.J.?" he called, "where are you?"

Right away, P.J. appeared at the bottom of the stairs. "Here I am. You ready?"

"No, not yet," Jeremiah answered.

"You need to hurry up and get ready so you can eat breakfast. My mom left the blue suit and stuff for you to wear on the chair."

"All right," Jeremiah answered.

"Oh, an' hurry up," P.J. yelled. "We're havin' pancakes!"

"Pancakes? I'll be right there!" Jeremiah managed to get himself washed up and dressed in record time. He put on the dark blue suit, crisp white shirt, and dark blue bow tie. There sitting on the floor was a pair of polished black leather shoes. Placing his feet inside, he winced because they were a little too tight, but when he turned around and got a glimpse of himself in the mirror, the slight discomfort immediately went away. Satisfied with his reflection, he grinned and gave himself a "thumbs up" to show his approval. For a moment, while standing in front of the mirror, he pretended he saw P.J. alongside him, while Mr. and Mrs. Kennedy posed proudly behind their two boys in what had to be the greatest family portrait ever taken.

It was the sound of Mrs. Kennedy's voice calling him to breakfast that brought Jeremiah back to reality. This was a reality he knew all too well. Every time he'd been placed with a family, he imagined himself staying with them forever. His dream had not come true in the past, and he wondered why this feeling of wanting to stay was so much stronger than any of those other times. In the past, something would go wrong, and his dream of finding a permanent home would very abruptly come to an end.

Maybe this time will be different, he thought. After all, Mrs. Kennedy already knew everything about him. There wouldn't be any surprises this time. They were 100 percent aware of what they were getting. But then again, he reminded himself, that could be the very thing to prevent them from taking him into their home. Jeremiah walked over to the window and stared down at the red maple. He desperately wanted to see signs of new life. "C'mon," he said. "Why don't you grow?"

His plea was interrupted when he heard P.J. once again yelling for him to come downstairs. "Hurry up, Jeremiah! I'm gonna eat *your* pancakes *and* mine!"

Jeremiah didn't need to hear another word. He tore himself away from the window and ran downstairs as fast as he could. When he reached the kitchen, Mr. Kennedy was about to have a cup of coffee. Mrs. Kennedy poured it into his cup, and he kindly told her thank you.

"Good morning, Jeremiah," they said cheerfully.

"Good morning," he said, sitting down and pushing his chair close to the table.

"My, you look handsome," said Mrs. Kennedy.

"Thank you," Jeremiah said, eagerly awaiting what he knew would be a scrumptious breakfast.

"Yeah," P.J. added as he laughed. "You almost look as good as I do."

Jeremiah felt real good stepping into the Kennedy kitchen. It had a warm and loving feeling about it, and just being there made him feel that same kind of warmth on the inside. Mr. Kennedy leaned over and gave him a cloth napkin. "Here," he said, helping him tuck it into his collar. "Put this in here so you won't get anything on your clothes." Jeremiah smiled when he saw Mrs. Kennedy coming toward the table with what looked like an enormous stack of golden brown pancakes. She placed two large pancakes on Jeremiah's plate and was surprised when she didn't get the response she'd anticipated.

Noticing but not understanding Jeremiah's look of disappointment, Mrs. Kennedy sought an explanation. "Is something wrong, Jeremiah? I thought you loved pancakes."

"I do, but I thought all those were mine."

Mr. and Mrs. Kennedy and P.J. laughed. "Well," said Mr. Kennedy, "let's see what you can do with those first, okay?"

"Okay," he agreed, as he poured on the syrup and speared his fork into his stack of steaming pancakes. "I can eat a million!"

By the time he finished the last bite of the second pancake, Jeremiah knew he was full. "No more for me; I'm full," he conceded.

"Well, I'm not!" P.J. said, grabbing the last pancake. He quickly spread some butter and poured syrup on it. To everyone's surprise, that pancake seemed to disappear even faster than the time it had taken him to pick it up. And when it was gone, his expression was clearly one of tremendous satisfaction.

"Next time," Jeremiah told him. In that second, he suddenly remembered there would be no next time. The seeds hadn't grown, and today was Sunday. From day one, he had hoped, wished, and prayed that he could stay with the Kennedys. And with Sunday already here, he knew with each passing minute that the chances of his prayer, his wish, and his dream coming true were becoming more and more remote. What he needed and hoped for now was something great and wonderful to happen that would change the course of his life. It would be something no one understood or could make sense of. Jeremiah knew he needed what Grandma Joanie had called "a miracle."

"You boys put your plates in the sink and wash your hands," Mrs. Kennedy told them. "We'll be leaving in ten minutes."

"How do I look, Mom?" P.J. asked, standing straight and

tall. His mother put her finger on her chin as though giving careful thought to her answer.

"Hmmm," she said, moving closer to her son so she could straighten his tie. "There, now you're ready. And you're looking real sharp. I'll be the envy of all the ladies at church walking in with three sharply dressed men," she said, straightening Jeremiah's bow tie as well. Everyone laughed.

The boys cleared their plates from the table, and after washing and drying their hands, left the kitchen. Mrs. Kennedy began washing the dishes and felt pleased about what she heard as they walked away.

Jeremiah gave P.J. a light rap on the arm. "You got a good mom, ya know."

P.J. tapped him back and spoke confidently. "I know."

The ride in the car was a short one. Jeremiah could hear the sound of voices singing as Mr. Kennedy pulled the car into the parking lot. As soon as they parked, a man walked up, put out his hand and greeted them. He had a deep hearty laugh, and when he said good morning, it sounded as though it had come from a place where words were rich and full of life. He tipped his hat. "Morning, Mrs. Kennedy!"

"Good Sunday morning to you too, Mr. Kirkwood," she said.

Mr. Kirkwood peered into the backseat. "Well, well, well . . . who do we have here?"

P.J. greeted him with a big grin. "It's me, Mr. Kirkwood, P.J.!"

"Oh, I know you, P.J., but who's this other big fella sittin' back there with you?"

"That's Jeremiah, and he's staying with us for the weekend."

"Glad to meet you, Mr. Jeremiah," Mr. Kirkwood said.

"Glad to meet you too," Jeremiah told him. "Who's singing?"

"That's the choir. And don't they sound fine as they can be this beautiful Sunday morning?"

Mr. Kennedy turned off the motor and looked directly at both boys and spoke firmly. "No playing around. I want you to listen and pay attention."

"We will," P.J. assured his dad. "Won't we, Jeremiah?"

"Yep. We'll be sure an' listen to every word."

Everyone got out of the car, and Mr. Kirkwood walked alongside Mr. and Mrs. Kennedy while the boys trotted a few steps in front of them. Approaching the clear glass doors, Jeremiah looked up and stared at the steeple that stood high on top of the building. "Man," he said, taking a big breath. "That's way bigger than the church me an' my grandma used to go to."

Jeremiah's soft brown eyes widened as he studied the huge structure. As though able to read his friend's thoughts, P.J. lightly tapped him on the arm. "It only looks real big from the outside," he assured Jeremiah. "Bet you're gonna find the same God waitin' on the inside."

The closer he got to stepping inside, the louder the music became, and Jeremiah hoped P.J. was right about God being there. He felt the music vibrating beneath his feet. It was happy and joyful, just the way he remembered when he had gone to church with his grandma. And little by little, his fears were leaving him. He was starting to think P.J. was right. The building that appeared gigantic in size from the outside was kind and inviting on the inside. As they entered, a woman with a glistening smile standing near the door cheerfully greeted them. "Good morning!" she said. "And welcome!"

Once again, Jeremiah could feel his special sense about people taking hold. He could hear his grandma reminding him. "The eyes, my child, are like mirrors. They can reflect kindness from the inside and pass that kindness on to others. When you look into the eyes of those you meet along life's way, always try to see something good." Jeremiah resolved that the lady at the door was indeed one of those "nice people." Her eyes were full of that kindness he'd learned to search for, and she had a beautiful smile to match.

Once the family was seated, P.J. began clapping his hands right away to the beat of the music but fell asleep the minute the sermon began. Mrs. Kennedy gave him a look that said somebody wouldn't be getting any dessert that evening. Jeremiah had tried a few times to nudge P.J., but nothing seemed to wake his friend from the comfortable deep sleep he had settled into.

There was a whole lot the preacher said that Jeremiah didn't understand, but he struggled to listen to every word. Maybe, he thought, *there will be an answer here*. It seemed as if all those words were swirling around in Jeremiah's head. Desperately, he tried to retrieve the ones he thought could be helpful. Finally, he settled on the only ones he could recall, ". . . ask and it shall be given unto you," the Reverend Garner encouraged. Jeremiah nodded his head yes to the accompaniment of the "Amens" and "yes sirs" coming from the congregation. But as far as he was concerned, this was a conversation between himself, Reverend Garner, and God. Certain that he had been given words of divine direction, he made up his mind. *That's what I need to do*, he thought. *I need to ask Mr. and Mrs. Kennedy if I can stay.* He decided that very instant that when the time was right, he would ask if he could live with them forever. The hard part, he knew, would be finding that right time to do it.

Later that evening as the family was finishing dinner, Jeremiah searched the faces and studied the eyes of Mr. and Mrs. Kennedy. He realized if ever there was a time to try to see hope in the eyes of another, it was now. Needing to recognize some sort of clue to let him know if he had chosen correctly, he began clearing his plate from the table. "I can wash the dishes if you want me to," he offered.

P.J. gave Jeremiah a look that questioned his offer. "Pssst!" he said while waving his hand to say *no*.

"Thank you, Jeremiah," Mr. Kennedy said. "Mrs. Kennedy and I would like to speak to you for a just a few minutes. After that, you and P.J. can tackle the dishes together."

"I'll wash, you dry!" P.J. was quick to call out.

Jeremiah walked back to the table and sat down. He could see that the Kennedys were serious, and it troubled him. He began going over in his head whether or not he had done something wrong. *How could the news be good,* he wondered, *when nobody is smiling?* He sat up in his chair as straight as he could and waited for someone to speak.

Mr. Kennedy cleared his throat and looked over at his wife. "Do you want to start?" he asked her.

She lightly patted him on the arm and replied, "No, you go ahead."

Jeremiah glanced over at P.J., who hadn't said a word. In fact, he seemed just as serious as his parents. However, his serious demeanor was for a different reason. He was hoping his parents had forgotten about his sleeping in church earlier that morning and wondered if they would let him have a piece of the delicious chocolate cake his mom had placed on the counter.

"Jeremiah, I know you haven't seen a whole lot of Mrs. Kennedy this weekend," Mr. Kennedy said, breaking the silence.

"Did I do something I shouldna, 'cause I . . ."

"No, Jeremiah you've been very good. She's been very busy making lots of phone calls and trying to get some answers to some really important questions."

He cautiously asked, "Questions about me?"

Mrs. Kennedy reassuringly put her arm around his small shoulders. "Yes, there were a few hard questions about you that needed to be answered."

Jeremiah found himself carefully wondering how to respond. *Couldn't they have simply asked me the things they wanted to know?* He would have gladly answered all of their questions. And who, better than he, would have the answers they needed?

Suddenly, Jeremiah thought about the Barkleys. He hadn't exactly been a model of good behavior when he lived with them. In fact, he had only been in their home for about forty-eight hours when on the second night, out of a deep sleep, he jumped out of his bed and began running all through the house. From that moment, he could tell they were afraid, and he understood that taking him back was just a formality. Then there were the Daniels, the couple who had returned him to "Children's Services" on Friday. Maybe they had called and shared with the Kennedys information about every time they had been summoned to the principal's office because of something he'd done.

However, none of this thinking made any sense, because Mrs. Kennedy had all of his information anyway.

Jeremiah could tell by the expressions on their faces that the Kennedys were bracing themselves to share some earth-shattering news. He glanced over at P.J. and searched his eyes for a tiny glimmer of hope. If he could see that, he knew at least there was a chance for him.

Mr. Kennedy looked over at his wife, then at P.J., and cleared his throat one more time. "It took a lot of work, but . . ."

Jeremiah couldn't sit still any longer. He jumped up out of his seat, ran out the front door, and headed up the street. He cupped his hands tightly over his ears and told himself as long as he kept running, he wouldn't have to hear the awful news. But he could hear the sound of Mr. Kennedy's voice calling after him. "STOP, JEREMIAH!"

He knew Mr. Kennedy was coming and would probably catch him. And when he did, he grabbed Jeremiah and held him firmly so he couldn't get away. "Jeremiah, you're a good runner, but if you only run away from something, you'll never reach or get to the good things waiting for you." This time, he looked directly into Jeremiah's eyes. "We'd like you to stay with us if you want to."

Jeremiah took his hands away from his ears and wiped the tears streaking down his face. Part of him couldn't believe the words he heard Mr. Kennedy say, yet he knew they were all too real. However, he still needed and wanted to hear them again. "Huh?" he asked gazing up at Mr. Kennedy.

P.J. and his mom came running, too. When they reached Jeremiah and Mr. Kennedy, they stood next to them. "Don't you get it?" P.J. asked. "You're gonna stay with us."

Jeremiah searched each of their faces and was pleased to see all three of them were silently speaking the same thing. "I can stay . . . really?"

"Really," Mrs. Kennedy said softly.

Although his mustard seeds hadn't grown, God had decided to answer the prayer of the one who had planted them. And while Jeremiah hadn't asked the Kennedys to let him stay, it seemed pretty clear they all had asked the One who was able to answer. Jeremiah Jones needed more than a place to stay; he needed a family. And today, the Lord had given him one.

Chapter 10

NO BUS, NO FUSS

MONDAY MORNING arrived quickly. Jeremiah opened his eyes to find the morning sun greeting him, and he welcomed it with gladness. For the first time in as long as he could remember, he looked forward to going to school. He turned over in the covers one more time, then got up, and made his way to the bathroom. Before he left the room, he looked out the window, and squinted his eyes, still checking to see if there was any evidence of the planting he'd done near the tree. Still feeling wonderful after hearing he could stay with the Kennedys, he clasped his hands together to make sure he hadn't dreamed this good news. He even convinced himself he saw something tiny sprouting from the earth right near the red maple tree.

As he made his way across the floor, he was careful not to step on P.J. Mr. and Mrs. Kennedy had explained he would be starting at a new school this morning, and as much as he had prayed to live with them, he knew his behavior in school could be the one thing to ruin his chances of staying with them for good. Whether it was fighting, running through the halls, or not listening to directions, somehow the situations that happened in school always played the biggest part in deciding whether Jeremiah got to stay or had to go. Clenching his fists and teeth tightly, he vowed that wouldn't happen this time.

As soon as he came back into the room, he began shaking P.J. "C'mon, get up!" he said, yanking the covers off of him.

P.J. immediately drew the covers over his head. "We got plenty of time."

"I don't wanna be late for the bus."

"No bus," P.J. said in a drowsy voice. "My dad'll take us."

Jeremiah knew P.J. couldn't have given him better news. The bus was certainly one of the places where many of his conflicts usually began. *At least,* he thought, *there won't be any chance of getting into trouble on the bus because this time I don't have to ride it.* This was really his first official day with the Kennedys, and he naturally wondered how his placement and finding a school had happened so quickly. He thought about asking, but instead decided the Lord had simply given him one of those "miracles" Grandma Joanie had talked about. Hearing there would be no bus ride just made his chance of staying put this time look that much brighter.

Mrs. Kennedy made the school lunches while the boys finished their breakfast. Jeremiah watched her cut the peanut butter and jelly sandwiches into funny shapes and admired how carefully she wrapped them. When she was done, she placed the sandwiches, followed by a piece of fruit and a small bag of chips, into the bags. The next thing the boys heard was the sound of Mr. Kennedy's blaring car horn signaling that it was time to leave.

"It's time to go!" P.J. said clearing away what was left of his breakfast. Jeremiah did the same. P.J. stepped over to his mom to get the hug he'd become accustomed to every morning.

"You too, Jeremiah, I wouldn't send you off to school on your first day without a hug." Jeremiah readily made his way over to Mrs. Kennedy. If hugs were being given out, he surely wanted his share. "Have a great day!" she said with lots of enthusiasm.

As soon as they heard the car horn for the second time, they hurried themselves outside and got into the car. "School's only a few minutes away!" P.J. said.

Jeremiah nodded his head and tried to look like he had everything under control. "That's good," he said, knowing his stomach had begun turning itself in tiny little knots.

For a few seconds he closed his eyes and tried to shake the image of seeing himself standing before Mr. Kelton, the principal from his last school, who, towering overhead reminded him, "You won't get away with this, this time."

But like a fresh breeze of air passing by, he heard the words, "God gives brand new chances every day." At that moment, Jeremiah declared he would accept *his* new day and all the brand new chances that came along with it.

P.J.'s calculation on the time for the ride was pretty exact. The Minton Day School was only minutes away from the Kennedy home. Mr. Kennedy drove down two, maybe three blocks from their house, turned left, drove another two blocks, made a right turn, stayed straight for one more block and they were there. Jeremiah wished the ride had been longer because he still wasn't quite sure he was ready.

Watching Mr. Kennedy as he carefully guided the car into the parking lot, Jeremiah reminded himself not to do any running. No matter how nervous he was feeling, he promised to do everything in his power to stay calm and quiet. This, he convinced himself, was the only way to guarantee he could live with the Kennedys forever.

Once Mr. Kennedy turned off the car, he turned around and looked at his two passengers in the backseat. "Well, we're here. Don't forget to take your lunches and anything else you'll need for today."

P.J. was the first to get out. "See ya, Dad, catch up with you later, Jeremiah," he yelled, as he quickly recognized two friends and headed off to join them walking into the building.

Jeremiah felt a little bit abandoned and faced the reality of fending for himself. Almost as though able to read his mind, Mr. Kennedy offered some reassurance. "P.J. didn't leave you. I told him since it's your first day, I'd be taking you inside."

Jeremiah wondered if any evidence of the gigantic sigh of relief he felt could be seen spilling over and revealed by the satisfied look on his face. "Really, Mr. Kennedy?"

"Sure thing, you come with me." Mr. Kennedy got out of the car and grabbed a black leather bag off the seat next to him. "Okay, let's go!" he said closing his car door.

Jeremiah quickly got out, closed his door, and began to walk cautiously and somewhat slowly beside Mr. Kennedy. Once inside the building, Mr. Kennedy walked directly into the main office.

He quickly read something, signed his name, and spoke softly to an older woman sitting behind a desk on the far side of the room. They exchanged polite good mornings, and he was directed to enter the door located directly behind her desk. Jeremiah figured she was probably the secretary, because Mrs. Flint at his old school also held the exalted position of "guarding" the mysterious door behind her desk that bore the words PRINCIPAL'S OFFICE.

Jeremiah began worrying that they might ask him to come in and listen to a long list of do's and don'ts designed to help him be successful at his new school. He found himself thinking about what possibly might be number four on the list, when the door flew open and out stepped Mr. Kennedy and a tall slender man who clearly looked too young to be the principal of a school. He stood straight, had mopping black hair, and politely smiled as the two men walked over to where Jeremiah was sitting. "You must be Jeremiah," he said pleasantly. "Welcome to Minton!"

Mr. Kennedy lifted his hand, signaling Jeremiah to stand up. "Jeremiah, this is Mr. Stanton, your new principal."

Mr. Stanton quickly stuck out his hand. "I forgot to shake your hand, Jeremiah. I always shake the hands of our new students. And let me say again, welcome!"

"Thank you," Jeremiah quietly responded. He longed to look into Mr. Stanton's eyes to see if he could detect some of that all important kindness he needed. But for some reason, he decided not to look for fear he might not find it. For now, he would have to be satisfied with the kindness he heard in his voice.

"Mr. Kennedy, if you don't mind, would you take Jeremiah around to room 109? I'm sure Mrs. Buford will be glad to meet him." Mr. Stanton leaned down and whispered to Jeremiah, "Have a really great first day."

"Thank you, Greg," Mr. Kennedy said to Mr. Stanton as he and Jeremiah left the office. When they stepped out into the hallway, they did so at exactly the same moment as the sounding of the first bell signaling the start of the school day. They immediately found themselves swarmed in the midst of hallway traffic. And as they maneuvered their way through the throngs of students, several waved and said hello to Mr. Kennedy.

Over and over again, the same words rang out. "Hi, Mr. Kennedy!" Jeremiah was impressed with the fact that every time one of those "hellos" was heard, right away Mr. Kennedy would return a good hearty "hello" right back.

Jeremiah studied the numbers on every door they passed. When they reached room 109 he found himself a little afraid to go inside. Mr. Kennedy could see that Jeremiah was nervous, so he put his hand on his shoulder. "Want me to go inside with you?" Jeremiah wanted to say yes, but he felt he needed to go in alone.

He shook his head no. "I'm okay," he said forcing a smile. "Have a good day," Mr. Kennedy told him. "And I'll see you later."

For a few seconds more, Jeremiah watched Mr. Kennedy as he walked back down the long crowded hall and continued looking until he was no longer in his sight. He looked to his left and to his right and when he thought no one was looking, he bowed his head and whispered, "Please God, let everything be okay." Then he went inside.

There seated behind a large oak desk was his teacher. Jeremiah was surprised that his new teacher was so young and pretty. She couldn't have been any more than twenty-five-years-old, and he wondered how much could someone so young really know about helping children? But the minute she stood up and so graciously welcomed him to room 109, he believed maybe he had just met the best teacher in the whole wide world.

The other students were quietly working at their seats when she called for their attention. Jeremiah's eyes scanned the room. He saw pictures and all kinds of artwork along with samples of good work posted on a huge bulletin board near the front of the classroom. At the very top of the bulletin board were big bright orange letters that spelled the word "SUPERSTARS." He secretly hoped in the days to come that maybe his teacher would hang up one of his papers too. "You must be Jeremiah," she said pleasantly.

"Yes," he said softly. "I am."

"Well, Jeremiah, I am Mrs. Buford, and I want to welcome you to our class."

Jeremiah was surprised to see that there were only ten students in the class, and now he would make the total number eleven. "You can put your things in the closet," she said, pointing toward the back of the room. "And your seat will be right here," she added, directing him to an empty desk that was near hers. He put his lunch on a shelf in the closet and walked to his seat. Having to sit so close to the teacher's desk made him feel uneasy. After all, he'd been placed near his teacher's desk before, and in no way did he consider it a good thing. *What did Mrs. Buford know?* he wondered. Maybe someone had told her about all the problems he'd had at his old school. And perhaps this was her way of letting him know she wasn't going to tolerate any misbehaving in her class.

He felt relieved that his predictions were wrong. The minute he sat down at his new desk, he was pleased to see his name had already been written across the top, and right in front of the "J" in Jeremiah and after the "J" in Jones, Mrs. Buford had put bright yellow happy-face stickers. Knowing he had been expected and that Mrs. Buford had made special preparations helped him feel like he was already part of her class.

"Class, please say hello to Jeremiah," Mrs. Buford encouraged.

"Hi, Jeremiah!" the other students called out with enthusiasm.

Jeremiah put up his hand and waved hello. What should have been just an ordinary wave turned into an excited greeting when he recognized one of the students in the room. It was Mike, P.J.'s friend from the track meet. The sight of a familiar face suddenly made him feel a lot more at ease. He found it interesting that Mike showed no evidence of the temper he displayed on Saturday when his team lost the relay race.

Mrs. Buford spent much of the morning working closely with Jeremiah and helping him with his math. It was his hardest subject, but he liked the way his teacher said, "Learn to conquer a task a little bit at a time, and it will never conquer you." He was determined not to let math or any other subject have the last word on his success.

He felt good in this class . . . real good. And just as he knew living with the Kennedys felt right in his heart, he also knew the Minton School was a place where he believed he could learn.

Chapter 11

GUESS WHO?

BY THE TIME ten o'clock came around, Mrs. Buford asked everyone to put their work away and get in line. Mike went directly to the front of the line, and the other students lined themselves up directly behind him. Jeremiah looked at a chart that was posted on the wall behind Mrs. Buford's desk and saw that Mike had the assigned duty of being class line leader for the week. "Jeremiah?" Mrs. Buford called out. "How do you feel about being the caboose?"

"Caboose?" he asked.

"Yes, for this week it will be your job to close the door when we leave. Is that all right with you?"

A simple one-word answer was all he gave. "Yes." Following that, Jeremiah took his place at the end of the line. And when Mrs. Buford gave the signal for Mike to begin walking, he completed his first duty as the "caboose" of room 109 and closed the door.

Mike led the class quietly down the hall, past the main office, and continued walking until he stood in front of two large brown wooden doors. Jeremiah may not have been the best reader in his old school, but he immediately recognized the word painted on the door. In bold black letters was the word Gym, and he wondered how this day could get any better. Gym class was Jeremiah's favorite subject because it was the only subject in school that not only allowed but encouraged everyone to make noise, jump, and run. Jeremiah thought, *Whoever invented gym class must have surely been a genius.*

Mrs. Buford waited with her class. "I'll be right there," a voice said coming from a little office way in the back of the room. Jeremiah thought the voice sounded familiar, but it wasn't until he saw the gym teacher emerge from that little office room that he found himself able to say only one word.

"Wow!" he exclaimed. Not wanting to give even the slightest inkling that he couldn't control himself, Jeremiah quickly put his hand over his mouth and remained quiet. After getting a good look at his teacher, he was speechless and surprised that even his one word comment had been able to break through. As unbelievable as one might have thought it to be, there standing in front of the class with his whistle around his neck and a bright smile greeting every face was none other than Mr. Kennedy. *He* was the gym teacher at Minton Day School, and for Jeremiah Jones, who had wondered how this day could get any better, the answer to his question had just become evident. And now he understood why so many students had called out to Mr. Kennedy as the two of them walked through the halls earlier that morning.

The students quickly went to their assigned places on the

floor, and Mrs. Buford left. "Jeremiah, you can stand right here," Mr. Kennedy said, pointing to a space behind a tall boy wearing a blue T-shirt. While Mr. Kennedy was checking the attendance roster, another teacher soon appeared in the doorway, and she too had about ten students who entered and hurriedly took their places on the floor.

"Sorry, Mr. Kennedy, they needed a little more time to finish a test," she said.

"No problem," he said. "We were just about to start. Okay, everyone take your places." While anxiously waiting for class to begin, Jeremiah found himself in for yet another surprise. Walking in last and slowly finding his place on the floor was none other than George Radcliff from the track team. Jeremiah made an interesting observation. *I saw Mike, now George, and I rode with P.J., so Ronnie the other boy from the track team must be around here somewhere too*. He scanned the room as quickly as his eyes would allow but didn't have any success locating him. For now, though, he was happy knowing he'd get to see P.J., George, Mike, and Mr. Kennedy every day!

The sound of Mr. Kennedy's whistle brought Jeremiah back to the present. First they completed their warm-up exercises, and he made sure he kept up with every stretch, every jumping jack, and every knee bend the class was directed to do. Then Mr. Kennedy had everyone get into one big line and run around the entire gym three times. For Jeremiah, running around the gym was the best part of the whole period. After the run, Mr. Kennedy divided the class into four smaller groups and began explaining some of the fundamentals of basketball. He made sure every person got a chance to block, shoot, and dribble. Jeremiah liked the way Mr. Kennedy was so fair minded and encouraging to his students.

He and George were in the same group for this part of the lesson, while Mike was in another group. Jeremiah wanted to ask George if he remembered him but decided he would get around to asking him later. *Right now,* he reminded himself, *nothin' is more important than following Mr. Kennedy's instructions.*

Just then, he could feel someone nudging him on his arm. "You remember me?" Jeremiah turned around and saw that it was George. He was at the end of the line waiting for a turn to shoot the basketball.

One of the students bounced the ball to George. It was his turn to shoot, but he seemed more interested in talking to Jeremiah. "You're the one that was with P.J. at the track meet, right?"

"Yeah," Jeremiah said proudly. He was pleased that George remembered him.

"You go to school here now?"

"Yeah, I'm gonna be stayin' with the Kennedys for a while." He could tell George wanted to ask something else, but Jeremiah really didn't feel like talking about himself. George took a deep breath and hurled the ball straight up into the air. "Gonna be on the track team?"

"I dunno . . . maybe."

George stood staring up at the basket, as though somewhat annoyed that with all the effort he'd put into his throw, it didn't even come close to going in. "That's okay, George!" Mr. Kennedy yelled. "You keep at it, and you'll make it."

Mr. Kennedy's words brought a smile to George's face. And by the way he tossed the ball to the next shooter and headed back to the end of the line, it was obvious that the next time he came up, he would try harder. And eventually, just as Mr. Kennedy said, he'd probably shoot that ball right through the hoop.

On the second go round, George passed the ball to Jeremiah. Jeremiah stood at the foul line just the way Mr. Kennedy had demonstrated to the class and stared at the basket way too long. Some of the other kids in line had begun shouting, "Shoot the ball!" Jeremiah tossed it as high as he could, but the ball hit the floor pretty far off from what was considered near the basket. In fact, he hung his head, knowing that his shot wasn't even close.

"Keep up the good work!" Mr. Kennedy called out. Jeremiah grinned and just like George took his place at the end of the line anxiously waiting to get another chance.

George turned around and put up his hand to give Jeremiah a high five. "That was pretty good."

"Think so?" Jeremiah asked.

"Just a little harder throw and it woulda went right in."

"Yeah?"

"Oh, yeah," George said.

"Thanks."

Mr. Kennedy loudly blew his whistle and everyone returned to their places on the gym floor. Soon, both Mrs. Buford and the other teacher who had left her class appeared in the doorway together, ready to pick them up. As soon as Mr. Kennedy gave a signal for them to move, the students formed a line near their teachers. George waved as he attached himself to the end of the line. "See ya, Jeremiah, see ya, Mike!"

"See ya," Jeremiah replied.

"Yeah," Mike said looking away, "see ya."

Jeremiah couldn't understand why Mike didn't seem to like George very much. From what he could see, George seemed pretty friendly and liked to laugh. When Mr. Kennedy split the larger group into four smaller ones, he knew what he was doing putting Mike and George on opposite teams. Jeremiah remembered to take his place at the end of the line and followed his class back to room 109. As he was leaving, he waved to Mr. Kennedy, who winked, smiled, and waved back.

Later, while on his way to lunch, Jeremiah got one more surprise. As his class entered the cafeteria, another class was leaving. There standing in the fourth spot in line of the other class was Ronnie, the final member of the track team. And now the whole picture was complete. It was good to know that everyone on the track team attended Minton. And maybe Jeremiah's chances of getting on the team would be a little easier. He waved at Ronnie, but Ronnie didn't notice and proceeded to walk out the door with his class. For now, it was good enough just to know the team was there. *Tomorrow,* he thought, *I'll say hi again.*

Jeremiah sat at the lunch table with Mike but was curious because Mike had very little to say. He decided to try and start up a conversation. "Mr. Kennedy's the best, right?"

"The best what?" Mike asked sarcastically.

"The best gym teacher and track coach."

Mike acted as though he really didn't want to talk to anyone. "If you say so," he said, "even if we do lose all the time."

Jeremiah didn't want to do anything to make Mike's bad mood any worse. "I bet your team's gonna win the next one."

"How we gonna do that when we got George?"

Now Jeremiah could see why Mr. Kennedy made sure Mike and George weren't on the same team in gym. Mike had made up his mind that their team was never going to win as long as George Radcliff was a part of it.

Mike waited a little while before he said anything else, but it was pretty clear how much he wanted to be on a winning track team.

"You stayin' at P.J.'s?"

"Yeah."

"Did you ask Mr. Kennedy yet?"

"About what?" Jeremiah asked.

"About running with us."

"No . . . I didn't," Jeremiah said shyly.

"Bet if you ran with us we'd win." Knowing Mike wanted him to be a part of the team felt pretty good, but at the same time, it made Jeremiah feel bad knowing how much he wanted George off. "If you want me to, I'll ask 'im for ya," George said.

"That's okay, I can do it."

"Just make sure you ask 'im soon. We've got another meet comin' up, and maybe we'll come in first for a change," Mike said wistfully.

"Yeah . . . maybe."

When the school day ended, Jeremiah met P.J. and Mr. Kennedy in front of the school, and the three of them walked to the car. "How was your day, boys?" he asked.

"Good . . . real good," P.J. answered.

"And how about yours, Jeremiah?" Mr. Kennedy asked.

"It was the best! I think I like this school a lot, Mr. Kennedy. I like it a whole lot."

SOMETHING GOOD

AS FAR AS JEREMIAH was concerned, living with the Kennedys was wonderful. He looked forward to getting up each day and attending school, and he felt proud that in the two weeks he'd been at Minton, there hadn't been any phone calls, discipline reports, or homework notices sent home. Things couldn't have been better.

And while at times he felt anxious, he was overjoyed at being able to curtail his urge to run. There were a couple of times when he could almost hear himself saying *no* on the inside. And he reminded himself about what Mr. Kennedy had said about using his energy to run toward something rather than using it to run away. Jeremiah believed that advice helped, because those first two weeks had passed and he had been successful.

This particular morning Jeremiah was surprised to find that his school day routine had changed. As he and P.J. finished their cereal, Mrs. Kennedy told them to hurry because it was time to leave. Both boys seemed a little confused by the change, but nevertheless hurried to finish what was left in their bowls and cleared their dishes off the table.

"You're takin' us to school, Mom?" P.J. asked.

"Yes, and we need to hurry. I don't want you to be late."

"Is Mr. Kennedy all right?" he asked her.

Mrs. Kennedy could see Jeremiah was concerned and tried to reassure him.

"Mr. Kennedy is fine. He has something very important to do today. Don't worry. The three of you will be riding together again tomorrow. I promise."

The boys grabbed their lunches, got into the car, and Mrs. Kennedy drove them to school. Jeremiah thought she looked fine and found her to be her usual cheerful self, but he was still troubled because he hadn't seen Mr. Kennedy that morning.

When they reached the school, Mrs. Kennedy drove right up to the front entrance.

"Have a great day!" she said smiling pleasantly.

"Bye, Mom!" P.J. said, exiting the car.

Jeremiah closed the back door and got out too. "Bye, Mrs. Kennedy! You have a great day, too!"

Mrs. Kennedy watched the boys as they entered the building and then drove off. Both headed for the main door, and once inside, each went his own way. Already halfway down the hallway, P.J. called out to Jeremiah. "See ya later, okay?"

"Yeah, okay!"

When Jeremiah got to room 109, he was surprised to see that something else had changed. There was a tall man with a funny mustache sitting behind Mrs. Buford's desk. And with the class roster in one hand and the seating chart in the other, he had already started taking attendance. "You must be . . . uh . . . Jeremiah Jones," he said looking at the seating chart.

"Yes," Jeremiah answered politely but offered no other information. He wondered where Mrs. Buford was and hoped she'd be coming back real soon. How interesting he thought it was that she wasn't there. Usually, *he* was the person who'd show up and then in a matter of days would be gone. He liked this class, and he needed Mrs. Buford to come back.

Once the attendance was done, the tall man stood up and addressed the class. "My name is Mr. Porter, and I will be substituting for Mrs. Buford today."

In that one sentence, Jeremiah heard what he needed to hear, and felt relieved knowing his teacher would return the next day. Mr. Porter began walking around the room passing out manila folders to the students and soon was handing one to Jeremiah. Each folder had the student's name written across the top, and class work assignments for the day were on the inside.

Mr. Porter then positioned himself in the middle of the room to make sure everyone could hear. "These are the assignments Mrs. Buford left for you. If you have any difficulty, I'll be more than happy to help."

Jeremiah opened his folder. "Thank you," he said, turning over each page one at a time. He smiled confidently when he knew finishing the work wouldn't be a problem.

Mike had also opened his folder and started to work, but seemed to be having a hard time with the very first page. "I need help!" he called out. And right away, Mr. Porter hurried over to

Mike's desk and began explaining how to do the math problems that were giving him so much trouble. In a few minutes Mike was ready to tackle the rest of the worksheet on his own. "That's easy!" he said. "I can do it now."

Mr. Porter then went from desk to desk asking the other students if they needed his help with their assignments. By the time he returned to the front of the room, he was pleased to see everyone working.

Suddenly, out of nowhere, there was a loud noise that grabbed the attention of the entire class. Mike had become frustrated and slammed his math book on the floor. "I can't do this stuff—it's too hard!" he said loudly. He then took the paper, ripped it into as many little pieces as he could and threw them on the floor. Mr. Porter quickly went over to him, leaned down, and began speaking to Mike softly. Though the other students tried to hear what Mr. Porter was saying, they couldn't. But they did know whatever he had said must have been the right thing because after a few seconds, Mike picked up all the tiny pieces of paper, threw them into the trash can, and politely asked Mr. Porter for another page. This time, when he began his work, he finished it without any further disruption.

Jeremiah was glad they weren't scheduled to have gym class that morning because he knew Mr. Kennedy was not in school that day. And while Mr. Porter had proven himself to be more than capable as a substitute, Jeremiah and his classmates just wanted their regular teachers back.

By the time lunchtime came, everything seemed to be turning around for the better. It was Pizza Day, and that made all of the students happy. Jeremiah sat with Mike and another boy from his class named Aaron. Aaron hardly ever talked, but he amazed others with his exceptional ability to add and subtract so easily. He could take big columns of numbers and do all of the calculating in his head. Jeremiah's attention was captured just watching Aaron use his special skill. He had never seen anyone so young with such exceptional mathematical skills. He made working with numbers look simple; however, nothing else came as easy for him. He didn't run, he didn't play, and he rarely spoke. Jeremiah wondered if Aaron would willingly trade his gift for numbers for a day of laughing, talking, and running with his classmates.

At dismissal time, Jeremiah and P.J. were shocked to see Mr. Kennedy waiting behind the wheel of his car. "Let's go, you guys!" he called out.

They made sure they had all of their belongings and raced to get to the car.

"I won!" P.J. declared. "That means I get the front seat!"

"This time," Jeremiah conceded. "This time."

"Well, it looks like you two had a good day at school!" Mr. Kennedy said. Jeremiah and P.J. got into the car and from the minute Mr. Kennedy put the car in motion, Jeremiah and P.J. took turns telling about their day. Jeremiah shared that Mrs. Buford had been absent and how Mike had a rough time at first. "He'll be okay," Mr. Kennedy said. "Sometimes he gets a little scared when things change and he's not ready." Jeremiah nodded his head *yes*, knowing he understood what Mr. Kennedy said better than anyone.

As Mr. Kennedy pulled the car into the driveway, the boys were surprised to see Mrs. Kennedy standing out front waving.

It was unusual for her to be home so early in the day, so they figured something interesting must have been happening. "Hurry up," she said holding the door open.

P.J. and Jeremiah barely let Mr. Kennedy turn off the engine before the two of them leaped out, grabbed their book bags and headed straight for where Mrs. Kennedy was standing.

"Hi, Mom," P.J. said giving her a hug.

"Hi, Mrs. Kennedy." Jeremiah said, stepping up to give her a hug too.

"Hello, boys."

Mr. Kennedy got out of the car and walked up to the front door as well. He gave his wife a kiss and smiled. "Did you tell 'em?"

She returned his smile and shook her head *no*. "I wanted to wait so we could tell them together."

"What is it?" P.J. asked excitedly.

Jeremiah was anxious to know, too. "Is it something good? Will we like it?"

Mrs. Kennedy looked over at her husband. "Guess we'll just have to show them, won't we?"

He took her by the hand, started walking up the stairs, and signaled for the boys to follow. "I guess we *will* have to show 'em!" Mr. Kennedy said, winking his eye.

The boys followed them and gave one another a bewildered look. Checking for changes as they walked up the stairs, they couldn't detect anything different. From where they stood, everything was just as it had been when they left for school that morning. Not able to withstand the suspense any longer, Jeremiah broke the silence. "Please tell us what it is!" he pleaded.

"Yeah," P.J. joined in. "I can't take it anymore!"

Mr. and Mrs. Kennedy stopped in front of P.J.'s bedroom door. The boys were sure whatever the surprise was, it was behind that door. Mrs. Kennedy couldn't help smiling, and when Jeremiah and P.J. looked at Mr. Kennedy, he was smiling too. "Are you two ready for the surprise?" he asked.

"Yes," they both said in unison.

When Mr. and Mrs. Kennedy opened the door of P.J.'s room, the boys knew their surprise was as special as they had been led to believe. Their eyes lit up in amazement at what they saw. "Wow!" P.J. yelled.

"I don't believe this!" Jeremiah hollered. P.J.'s old bed was gone, and now in its place were brand-new, pecan-colored bunk beds: one for P.J. and one for Jeremiah.

"Man!" P.J. exclaimed thrusting himself onto the bottom one. "Bunk beds!"

"Can I have the top?" Jeremiah asked.

"Yeah," P.J. answered. "You can have the top."

As soon as Jeremiah heard those words, he dropped his book bag on the floor and climbed the small ladder that took him to the top. He let himself drop onto the bed, and while he lying on his back, he was pleased that the same soft mattresses and pillows that had been so much a part of P.J.'s old bed were now part of the new beds too.

Mr. and Mrs. Kennedy stood in the doorway. "Like the surprise?" she asked.

"It's the best!" Jeremiah squealed as he sat up.

"Yeah," P.J. agreed sticking out his head from the bed below. "This is the best room ever!"

Everyone was pleased with the new furnishings that now adorned P.J. and Jeremiah's room. Perched high atop his new bed, Jeremiah could see the whole room, and he liked what he saw. "Ya like *our* room?" P.J. asked.

"Yeah," Jeremiah answered. "I like our room a lot."

He interrupted his moment of relaxation and climbed down the little ladder, walked over to the window, and looked out into the backyard. Again, his eyes searched for any further growth in his little plant. Even if he couldn't see anything, he believed something good must have been happening in heaven. After all, as his grandma said, "faith was believing even when you couldn't see what you were hoping for."

"Everything all right?" Mr. Kennedy asked.

"Yeah," Jeremiah answered. "Everything's good." For a few more seconds, he stared out the window toward the red maple. In that moment, he remembered Grandma Joanie's *"strong special words"* . . . "Good things come to those who wait on the Lord." He didn't have to wonder or guess who had sent him this wonderful day. He knew that God had heard his prayer and believed He had also rewarded his mustard seed faith.

Chapter 13

ROOM FOR ONE MORE

ANOTHER TWO WEEKS had quickly flown by, and for each one of those weeks Jeremiah had faithfully accompanied Mr. Kennedy and P.J. to track practice on Mondays, Wednesdays, and Fridays. Sitting patiently and waiting on the bleachers was getting harder and harder with each practice session. No matter how hard he tried to extinguish the burning desire in his heart to run with the team, he couldn't. In fact, going to the track field only made the desire to run grow stronger.

Twice, the thought of asking Mr. Kennedy for a spot on the team had crossed his mind, but Jeremiah didn't want to risk doing anything that might put him on the bad side of the other runners. He didn't want it to look as if he was getting special treatment. He wanted the other runners to want him on their team. If they were willing to make room for him it would make his place on the track team all the more special in his eyes.

Jeremiah watched from the bleachers as Mr. Kennedy called for the team to gather around. He blew his whistle loudly one time and directed the boys to begin their stretching exercises. *I can do that,* he assured himself. *I can do that, and I can run fast. I just want a chance to run too.*

Mr. Kennedy blew his whistle a second time, signaling to get his team's attention. He noticed that Mike hadn't shown up and was missing doing his stretching with the others. This was a reason for concern because he knew how much Mike enjoyed running in the races. And everyone else on the team also knew he was probably the best runner they had. "Has anyone seen Mike?" Mr. Kennedy asked.

Sitting on the ground, lifting his arms, and reaching to touch his toes, George called out. "He'll be here! Mike never misses practice."

As soon as George said that, Jeremiah noticed a car pulling into the parking lot. It looked like Mike's mother's car, but from where he stood, it was hard to tell. However, once the car door opened, the mystery was solved. It was Mike, and he was coming to share some news, news that he wouldn't be running with the team today or for some days to come. Mr. Kennedy and the boys watched as Mike's mom got out of the car first and then opened the door for her son. When he slowly stepped out of the car, she reached into the backseat and brought out a pair of crutches. After helping him position himself properly on the crutches, she slowly walked alongside him while he made his way over to Mr. Kennedy and the rest of the team.

When Mike reached them, he slightly lowered his head because he wasn't ready to come face to face with the disappointing news he was about to deliver to his teammates. Finally, he took a deep breath and allowed the words he dreaded to come out of his mouth. "I can't run, Mr. Kennedy."

"He took a fall from his skateboard," his mother explained, "and sprained his ankle. The doctor said he'll have to be on crutches at least a week."

Mike was clearly disappointed, and his soft-spoken tone affirmed that. "Sorry, everybody."

Mr. Kennedy responded kindly. "It's okay, Mike. I know how much fun skateboarding can be." Though everyone suspected Mr. Kennedy was just as disappointed as the others on the team, his words were still encouraging. "I hope you'll feel better real soon and be ready to run again."

Hearing that seemed to take away the guilt Mike was feeling. You could see the difference those words made all over his face. He lifted his head and promised he would do what he could to help the team. Mike was quick to ask Mr. Kennedy about the dilemma facing them. No one else even dared ask it, because no one on the Blue Team wanted to hear the words spoken out loud. "But what about the meet coming up on Saturday? What are we gonna do?"

Mr. Kennedy looked at the faces of the boys on his team. And as good as he was when it came to offering encouragement and saying the right words, he found himself at a loss. The boys looked at one another as though acknowledging the trouble they were in since they would have to compete without their best runner. Suddenly P.J. blurted out a suggestion that he saw as a possible solution to their problem. "Let Jeremiah run with us," he said, pointing toward the bleachers.

George instantly agreed with P.J.'s idea. "Yeah, let Jeremiah run!"

Mr. Kennedy pushed back his cap off his forehead just a little. P.J. had learned this was a sign that his dad was giving serious thought to something. As the team's coach, it was important for him to know how all his runners felt if a change was going to be made. So for the moment, he centered his attention on Ronnie who had given no indication of how he felt about P.J.'s proposal. "What do you think, Ronnie? Should we ask Jeremiah to run in Mike's place on Saturday?"

Ronnie studied the faces of his teammates. He hadn't exactly been nice to Jeremiah and knew asking him to help was going to be hard. Ronnie had not given his opinion because he had already figured Jeremiah would say no. After all, what else could his answer be? Ronnie hadn't been nice to him from the day they met, and he knew what he had to do. He walked over to where Jeremiah was sitting on the bleachers and, standing before him, put out his hand for him to shake. "Will you run with us on Saturday, Jeremiah?"

Jeremiah had difficulty speaking but not because he planned to turn Ronnie down. It was because he was amazed that the second thing he had hoped and prayed for was happening. And without taking any time to think, the word "Yes" raced up his throat and leaped out of his mouth. So many times while watching the practices, he wanted to get up from the bleachers and dart out onto the track, just to see what it felt like to have that smooth wooden baton placed in his hand. Finally, after all those times seeing the others run and pass on that baton, Jeremiah Jones was going to get his chance. He had lived running with this team on the inside ever since the first time he'd witnessed them in a race.

What other answer was there to give? Clearly, "yes" was the only one possible. Allowing the word to spill out of his mouth a second time, he yelled it loud and clear. "YES!" Jeremiah exclaimed. "I wanna run with you!"

He and Ronnie ran over to where Mr. Kennedy and the rest of the team stood. The huge smile on Ronnie's face gave advance notice of the good news he was about to share. "He said he'll run! That's if it's okay with you, Mr. Kennedy."

Mr. Kennedy in turn, looked over at Mike, and when Mike nodded his head *yes*, Mr. Kennedy was pleased. "It looks to me like there's room for one more on the team. What do the rest of you guys say?"

"YES!" they answered together.

"All right!" said P.J. "Let's do this!"

After hearing P.J.'s declaration George stepped forward.

"Uh oh," Ronnie mumbled. "Here it comes. Ol' George probably wants to be the lead runner."

George heard Ronnie's comment but decided to ignore it. "Mr. Kennedy? Ya think we could call ourselves something besides the Blue Team?"

"Yeah," P.J. chimed in. "We need a better name."

"Somethin' like the Flying Leopards!" Mike suggested.

Without any explanation, Jeremiah took off and headed toward the bleachers. He grabbed something and quickly ran back to the team shouting. "I've got a name! We can be the Also Rans! Like this book!" He pointed at the beautiful stallion on the cover and showed it to everyone. "See, the title is *He Also Ran*. We're kinda like the story! He wanted to win a race, too, but he didn't. But by the end of the story people came from all over to see him run just because he never gave up." Jeremiah took a deep breath. "An' we're not givin' up either."

"You're right, Jeremiah," Mike supported. "We're not gonna give up. Our team's gonna run whether we win or lose."

Mr. Kennedy once again pushed his cap back from his forehead just a little bit more and proposed the question to the team. "Whatta you think? . . . Also Rans?"

"Also Rans," said Mike.

"Sure," said George.

"That's cool," said P.J.

Ronnie waited a few seconds before answering. "Also Rans . . . I like it! Yes."

"Then Also Rans it is," said Mr. Kennedy. "We may be the only ones who'll know what the name means, but we'll wear it with honor."

"Okay, you guys," Mike said. "On the count of *three*, let's shout it out as loud as we can. One, Two, Three . . ."

And every one of them, including Mr. Kennedy and Mike's mom, all yelled their name together: *"ALSO RANS!"*

Chapter 14

THEY ALSO RAN!

THE WEEK THAT followed seemed like the fastest week of Jeremiah's young life. Every day after school he practiced with the team and thought of nothing but running in the big race on Saturday. When he wasn't thinking about running, he *was* running.

In the days leading up to the race, he only wanted to talk about what he imagined as his "take off," when the referee signaled the start of the race by firing his pistol. Jeremiah had surely lost count of the number of times he'd already run that race in his mind. Each time he did, he thought of something to do that might make him a faster and a better runner. Even after practice, he did his leg lifts, knee bends, and trotted around the backyard maybe five or six times, hoping his extra effort would make a difference in the outcome.

With the race only days away, he found himself eating, sleeping, and drinking nothing but the big race. And he was determined nothing was going to stand in the way of his making his best possible run on Saturday. Even when P.J. tried to get him to play catch, he chose to run around the yard instead. Surprisingly, P.J. didn't question Jeremiah's choice. Instead, he put down his ball and glove and decided to run with him.

They had missed only one day's practice, and that was on Wednesday, the day it rained all day long. And Jeremiah would have probably gone out to run on that day too if Mr. and Mrs. Kennedy hadn't said it wasn't a good idea. He had become like the stallion in the story. He knew the importance of being persistent, and he wanted to try and do his best. Knowing if he did his part and finished the race, there was nothing he could be but a winner.

By the end of the week, Jeremiah felt he was prepared for Saturday. So much so that he and P.J. were up early and ready to get going even before Mrs. Kennedy had a chance to call them. All the way down the stairs, they were giving each other high fives as though this was their own special way of boosting their confidence.

"Think we're gonna win?" P.J. asked.

It only took Jeremiah a second to answer P.J.'s question. "I know we're gonna win!"

P.J. stopped when he got to the bottom step and turned around. "How ya know?"

Jeremiah smiled confidently. "Because I do."

Satisfied with Jeremiah's answer, P.J. smiled, too. It was just what he needed to hear. If Jeremiah could believe the Also Rans were going to win the race, then so could he.

When they entered the kitchen, they saw Mrs. Kennedy had

made a very special breakfast, pancakes. "Take a seat, boys," she said. She brought a steaming hot platter of pancakes and set them in the center of the table. She took a smaller plate and counted three pancakes and placed them there. "Jeremiah, here's a nice big stack to start you off."

"Thank you, Mrs. Kennedy, but I can't."

Mr. and Mrs. Kennedy were surprised. After all, pancakes were Jeremiah's favorite meal. "Are you all right?" she asked stopping to feel his forehead. "He doesn't have a fever," she said, looking at Mr. Kennedy.

"I can't have any either," P.J. said with conviction.

"Now I know something's wrong," said Mr. Kennedy. "If these boys are giving up the chance to have pancakes, something isn't right."

Jeremiah and P.J. stood up, each nudging the other to speak. After enough coaxing Jeremiah spoke first. "We don't want to get too full before we run."

"Yeah," P.J. supported. "The pancakes will weigh us down . . . an' we wanna win!"

"Well," said Mrs. Kennedy, "you don't have to eat pancakes, but you're at least going to have some cereal."

The boys looked over at Mr. Kennedy, who nodded in agreement.

"Okay," they said, sitting themselves back down in their seats. They were actually glad that they were told they had to eat something. Neither of them had looked forward to the notion of running on empty stomachs. Mrs. Kennedy passed them the box, and they filled their bowls so they could begin eating right away. "Slow down," she said, "you've got plenty of time."

"I'm not eating fast because of the race," Jeremiah told her. "I'm eating fast because I'm hungry."

"Well, slow down anyway," warned Mr. Kennedy. "We don't want you getting sick before the race either." Looking over at P.J., he gave the same warning. "That goes for you too, P.J., take your time."

Right away, he deliberately decreased the speed of his spoon as it moved toward his mouth. "I will."

Even though they followed Mr. and Mrs. Kennedy's advice to slow down, they still finished their breakfast in record time. No one had to remind either of them to clear their places. As soon as the last spoonful of cereal was eaten, they jumped up with their empty bowls, went over to the sink, and washed them.

"We're ready, Dad!" P.J. said speaking for himself and Jeremiah.

"Got everything you need?"

P.J. checked Jeremiah, and Jeremiah checked P.J. They made sure they were wearing their track shoes, shorts, and shirts. "Yes, Mr. Kennedy," Jeremiah said eagerly, "We're ready!"

When Mr. and Mrs. Kennedy found themselves pleased with the condition of the kitchen, they and the boys got into the car and headed for the track. All the way, Jeremiah kept looking down at his brand-new track shoes. They were white leather with thin blue stripes along each side. If ever there was a pair of shoes that had *winner* written all over them, it had to be the ones Jeremiah was wearing on his feet.

"Look!" P.J. yelled, pointing across the field as their car pulled into the track's parking lot. "Everybody's here already, just like they said . . . even Mike's here early, and he's not even runnin.' "

"He may not be running today, but he's still an important part of the team," Mr. Kennedy noted.

"Do your best, you two," Mrs. Kennedy told the boys as they exited the car. "I'll be cheering and watching every lap."

Jeremiah turned around and walked up to Mrs. Kennedy and gave her a hug. "We will. I'm gonna run like I never did before. You'll see."

P.J. came back to where his mom stood and gave her a hug, too. "We're gonna win today Mom! I can feel it."

"Even if you don't," she was quick to say, "be glad you were in the race."

That was an interesting thing to hear, Jeremiah thought. It reminded him of the times he'd heard his grandma telling him to slow down when he was rushing about all over the house. "A race is never won just because someone is fast," she'd say. "But the real winning crown in life goes to the one who lasts all the way to the end." Jeremiah knew what his prize would be that day, and P.J. was right. They *were* going to win if they could just run the entire race. The Also Rans needed to do something they'd never done before. They needed to *finish*. As pretty as all the ribbons adorning the judge's table looked, Jeremiah just wanted the whole team for once to cross the finish line.

Mr. Kennedy looked at his watch and realized they needed to get themselves over to line up with the rest of the team. "C'-mon, guys, let's get over to the starting area. The relay will be starting soon."

When they got there, George and Ronnie were stretching,

while Mike, crutches and all, stood over them keeping count. "C'mon, George, you can do it. Just five more knee bends and you're done."

"I don't know who's tougher," George moaned. "Mr. Kennedy or you."

"I vote for Mike." Ronnie laughed.

"Keep goin', Ronnie," Mike commanded. "You ain't finished either."

"Okay," Ronnie conceded ". . . seven . . . eight . . . nine, and ten! There, I'm done."

". . . Ten! I'm done too!" George said.

Mr. Kennedy spoke in his most encouraging voice. "You guys are looking great, like real winners . . . every one of you! And we'll win today."

"Think so, Mr. Kennedy?" Mike asked.

Every member of the team waited silently for Mr. Kennedy's answer. And as he searched their faces which were covered in nothing but hope, he gave the only answer he could. "Sure we will." Hearing those words from Mr. Kennedy made them want to try even harder to win than they'd planned.

The announcer called for the five teams scheduled to compete in the baton relay. Loud and clear he called, "The Also Rans in lane number three!" Just as they had practiced, Ronnie would start them off because next to Mike he was the fastest. The next runner would be P.J., who because of his limp sometimes had a tendency to slow down halfway around the track. George would run third, and everyone knew his position was critical. George was the one person on the team who had never finished a full lap around the track. The final runner was going to be Jeremiah, and he knew that once he felt that baton in his hand, holding on to it and maintaining the best pace he could might make all the difference in the world.

They lined up and, like each of the teams on either side of them, positioned themselves behind the first runner at the starting line and waited for the sound of the starting pistol. Hearing the announcer's voice give the count, signaled the team that the race was about to begin.

"On your mark . . . get set . . ." *Bang*! With the sound of the starting pistol, Ronnie took off like a rocket and ran with all his might. He started off with a good lead and made sure he held on tightly to the baton but began to get nervous when he glanced to his right and saw the runner in that lane slightly moving ahead of him. He remembered what Mr. Kennedy had told the team about "running their own race" and no one else's. For a moment, he wished he could close his eyes so he couldn't see the other runners but was relieved when he realized he was almost completely around the track, and found it was time to pass the baton on to P.J. The closer Ronnie got, the more he concentrated on making sure he would get that baton to the next runner.

P.J.'s eyes widened while he stood waiting anxiously for that all important pass. Ronnie kept up his speed, and just when it looked as if he was going to whiz right past P.J., everyone watched as the baton smoothly made its way into his hand. P.J. immediately started his leg of the run and never looked back. Before he knew it, he had made it all the way around the track. The runner in the fourth lane had taken the lead, but P.J. could hear his teammates cheering him on. "Go, P.J.! You can do it! Keep going!"

George got himself in position for what was about to be the third pass of the baton. He was ready to receive it as soon as P.J. came by and placed it neatly into his hand. George ran with it as fast as he could, but soon his lack of speed wasn't enough to keep up with any of the other four runners. In spite of all the effort Ronnie and P.J. had put into this race, the Also Rans watched themselves go from an honorable second place, to an okay third and finally back to their usual last place in a matter of minutes.

As George struggled to make his way around the track, he could feel the enthusiasm of only moments ago leaving him.

"C'mon, George! You can do it!" It was Mike encouraging him to keep going.

"All right, George!" Ronnie screamed. "Don't stop!"

George could feel his legs ordering themselves to buckle beneath him, while his brain commanded they keep moving. As though feeling an internal argument taking place between his brain and his legs, he was determined to cast the deciding vote in favor of his brain. Suddenly, he pushed himself harder and could feel the momentum he needed to make it all the way to where Jeremiah was standing. The sight of Jeremiah's hand sticking out was all the incentive George needed. When he was sure he was close enough, he quickly and successfully passed on the baton.

Jeremiah gripped it securely in his hand and ran faster than he could ever remember running before in his life. He could clearly see up ahead that one of the other runners had crossed the finish line. And it wasn't long after that he could see someone from another team crossing to capture second place.

Like a soft breeze gently carrying an inspiring message, Jeremiah could hear the words of his grandma once again. "The real winning crown belongs to the one who makes it all the way to the end." Jeremiah put all of his concentration into making it to the finish line. He could see himself gaining little by little on the boy in lane number five and felt a surge of energy come over him that caused his feet to move faster. His teammates were calling out loudly for him to keep going. With the finish line now clearly in his sight, crossing it was now nothing more than a formality. Just as he could feel his right foot touching down, the runner in the second lane crossed it only seconds before him. He could still hear his teammates and Mr. Kennedy yelling loudly. "Way to go, Jeremiah! That was great!"

Right away, he positioned himself at the end of the line with his team and put the baton in the hand of Ronnie who had been first. They listened as the announcer called out the names of the teams who had come in first, second, and third place in the event. Their team's name was not called, but for this race and on this day, they had *finished*.

"You boys were great!" Mr. Kennedy told his team.

"Yes, you were!" a voice said. Everyone looked around and were surprised to see that it was Mr. Radcliff, George's dad. He shook hands with Mr. Kennedy and said to the team, "Good run, guys! Good run!" He then walked over to George, put his arms around him, and gave him a warm hug. "I'm proud of you," he told him.

George looked his father in the eye and smiled. "I finished the race."

"I know you did, and that's what's important, son."

George stepped back just a little. "But we didn't win."

"Maybe you weren't first across the finish line, but the Also Rans definitely won something pretty important out there today. And you know what I think?"

George shook his head no while the others on the team quietly listened.

"Keep running with the kind of determination I saw, and soon, *real soon*, I bet you guys are going to come away with a ribbon. You're already in first place in my book!"

The boys on the team jumped up and down, hugged their coach, Mr. Kennedy, and hugged one another as though they had won a gold medal in the Olympics. And though Mike's voice was almost drowned out from the cheers coming from Mrs. Kennedy and all the people in the bleachers, his was still the loudest.

Jeremiah blended into the celebration, knowing his grandma's words were true. He could feel her *"strong words"* covering him lovingly all over. "God rewards those who trust Him and finish the race." And even though he knew the Also Rans would not receive a ribbon that afternoon, his heart was glad because they had finished the race set before them. And all who witnessed it, realized that on this day the Also Rans had been in the race too!

ISBN-10: 0-8024-0902-4
ISBN-13: 978-0-8024-0902-7

In this second book in the *Ricky and Friends* series, the kids are finding out the significance of being a missionary. In three different stories Ricky, Theo, Gina, and Clinton learn that being a missionary is a special calling from God that can be on anyone's life. This book combines fun stories with sound teaching on the need and reason for being a missionary, especially to Africa.

by Tony & Tracey Van Dyke
Find it now at your favorite local or online bookstore.
www.LiftEveryVoiceBooks.com

ISBN-10: 0-8024-2251-9
ISBN-13: 978-0-8024-2251-4

The girls of the Double Dutch Club have an opportunity of a lifetime: they're on their way to compete in a Double Dutch competition! What begins as a desire in their hearts to win a coveted trophy becomes the foundation for relationships that last a lifetime.

by Mabel Elizabeth Singletary
Find it now at your favorite local or online bookstore.

www.LiftEveryVoiceBooks.com

ISBN-10: 0-8024-2252-7
ISBN-13: 978-0-8024-2252-1

In the sequel to *Just Jump*, the girls from Grover Elementary return for the new school year only to learn that Ming, their wise leader, has returned to China with her family. They'll have to find someone else to jump Double Dutch with them in time for the December Jump Off. Meanwhile, Tanya and a new girl, Brittany, seem to keep bumping heads. And strong-willed Tanya is surprised to find the new girl can stand her ground in a fight. Join the adventure in book two of *The Double Dutch Club* series.

by Mabel Elizabeth Singletary

Find it now at your favorite local or online bookstore.

www.LiftEveryVoiceBooks.com

ISBN-10: 0-8024-8172-8
ISBN-13: 978-0-8024-8172-6

Carmen Browne is a ten-year-old African-American girl beginning fifth grade. With her family moving to a new city, Carmen is anguished to give up her friends and comfortable home. As her family adapts to a new location, Carmen learns that finding new friends and fitting in is not easy. Part of her doesn't even want to try. Family issues become complicated when Carmen's brother learns he is adopted. Dealing with unpopularity, fitting in, and cultural differences are Carmen's issues in the first book of the *Carmen Browne* series.

by Stephanie Perry Moore
Find it now at your favorite local or online bookstore.
www.LiftEveryVoiceBooks.com

The Negro National Anthem

Lift every voice and sing
Till earth and heaven ring,
Ring with the harmonies of Liberty;
Let our rejoicing rise
High as the listening skies,
Let it resound loud as the rolling sea.
Sing a song full of the faith that the dark past has taught us,
Sing a song full of the hope that the present has brought us,
Facing the rising sun of our new day begun
Let us march on till victory is won.

So begins the Black National Anthem, by James Weldon Johnson in 1900. Lift Every Voice is the name of the joint imprint of The Institute for Black Family Development and Moody Publishers.

Our vision is to advance the cause of Christ through publishing African-American Christians who educate, edify, and disciple Christians in the church community through quality books written for African Americans.

Since 1988, the Institute for Black Family Development, a 501(c)(3) non-profit Christian organization, has been providing training and technical assistance for churches and Christian organizations. The Institute for Black Family Development's goal is to become a premier trainer in leadership development, management, and strategic planning for pastors, ministers, volunteers, executives, and key staff members of churches and Christian organizations. To learn more about The Institute for Black Family Development write us at:

The Institute for Black Family Development
15151 Faust
Detroit, Michigan 48223

We hope you enjoy this book from Moody Publishers. Our goal is to provide high-quality, thought-provoking books and products that connect truth to your real needs and challenges. For more information on other books and products written and produced from a biblical perspective, go to www.moodypublishers.com or write to:

Moody Publishers/LEV
820 N. LaSalle Boulevard
Chicago, IL 60610
www.moodypublishers.com